BIG SHOT

Terry ran into Pat's arms and they embraced. The couple, with Nancy, Bess, and the Hardys, stood in the midst of a dense pack of reporters. Strobe lights flashed, TV floodlights glared, and a dozen journalists fired questions at Pat and Terry.

As she watched, Nancy froze in sudden shock. A hand emerged from the frenzied crowd, wearing a glove, but carrying neither a light nor a microphone.

Instead it held a pistol.

The pistol was a large-caliber automatic with an evil blue glint, capped with a bulbous silencer. It was pointed directly at Pat's chest!

Before Nancy could even open her mouth to shout a warning, the gloved hand squeezed the trigger. . . .

Nancy Drew & Hardy Boys SuperMysteries

Available from ARCHWAY Paperbacks

A NANCY DREW and HARDY BOYS SUPER·MYSTERY™

COURTING DISASTER

Carolyn Keene

AN ARCHWAY PAPERBACK
Published by POCKET BOOKS
New York   London   Toronto   Sydney   Tokyo   Singapore

This book is a work of fiction. Names, characters, places and incidents are either products of the author's imagination or are used fictitiously. Any resemblance to actual events or locales or persons, living or dead, is entirely coincidental.

AN ARCHWAY PAPERBACK *Original*

An Archway Paperback published by
POCKET BOOKS, a division of Simon & Schuster Inc.
1230 Avenue of the Americas, New York, NY 10020

Copyright © 1993 by Simon & Schuster Inc.
Produced by Mega-Books of New York, Inc.

ISBN: 0-671-78168-5

First Archway Paperback printing April 1993

10 9 8 7 6 5 4 3 2 1

NANCY DREW, THE HARDY BOYS, AN ARCHWAY PAPERBACK and colophon are registered trademarks of Simon & Schuster Inc.

NANCY DREW & HARDY BOYS SUPERMYSTERIES is a trademark of Simon & Schuster Inc.

Cover art by Frank Morris

Printed in the U.S.A.

IL 6+

COURTING DISASTER

Chapter

One

I CAN'T HEAR YOU!" Nancy Drew shouted across the café table at her friend Bess Marvin. Bess rolled her blue eyes at the group of teens who had just exploded in shrieks of laughter next to them.

The two friends were at a barbecue place called CJ's, which was filled with rowdy, vacationing students.

"Why did Kurt tell us to meet him here?" Bess yelled. "This place is a total madhouse!"

Nancy shrugged and smiled. "I guess they came here to have fun, like we did." She pulled her chair closer to Bess's, then gazed out at one of the beautiful streets of Charleston, South Carolina. The old pastel buildings faced with wrought iron balconies and flowering magnolias and azaleas made her feel as if she'd stepped back into the past. "Everywhere I look here there's a living history lesson."

Bess grinned, her eyes focused inside the restaurant. "Everywhere *I* look, I see awesomely cute guys, and some of them are gazing at us."

That figured, Nancy thought. Bess's curvy figure and pretty face framed by long blond hair attracted the interest of most boys.

"There'll be plenty of time for guys," Nancy said. At five feet seven, she was three inches taller than Bess and more slender. Her long reddish blond hair was pulled back into a high ponytail that poked out from a white tennis visor that had "Southern EXPOsure" printed on the bill.

Nancy wasn't interested in meeting new guys. She had a steady boyfriend back home—Ned Nickerson, a student at Emerson College. Spending time apart from Ned was the one drawback to this trip to the Southern EXPOsure festival with Bess.

The girls had been invited to the festival by Kurt Zimmer, an old friend of the Marvins. Kurt was directing a new rock musical, *Beauty and the Beat,* which was to open at the festival in a few days. It was starring Terry Alford, the most popular VJ on the country's top video channel, PTV.

Nancy and Bess were sorry that George Fayne, Bess's cousin and Nancy's other good friend, hadn't been able to join them.

According to Kurt, Southern EXPOsure had been a stuffy arts festival. The average age of people who came was about sixty. This year, the EXPO leaders had decided to go for a younger crowd, with music, theater, and other events aimed at students on spring vacation from college or high school. Judging by this first-day mob of kids, Nancy guessed that the strategy was working.

"It was terrific of Kurt to get us a room where the cast of *Beauty and the Beat* is staying," Bess commented. "I'm dying to meet Terry Alford, so I can find out where she gets those fantastic outfits she wears on TV."

Nancy laughed. "Do you remember that Terry was a child actress in that old TV sitcom 'Home with the Hendersons'?"

"Bess!" a deep voice cut through the noise. The girls turned toward a man wearing jeans and a faded T-shirt making his way toward them. A mane of wavy straw-colored hair framed his angular face and brown mustache. He was tall and thin, someplace in his early thirties.

"Kurt!" Bess jumped up and hugged the man, who then stepped back and grinned down at her.

"You've sure grown up in the last few years!" he said.

3

Bess blushed and smiled. "This is my friend, Nancy Drew," she said.

"I'm really looking forward to seeing your musical," Nancy said as he shook her hand. Just then she noticed a guy and girl standing behind Kurt. Kids were openly staring and pointing at them.

"Terry Alford!" Bess exclaimed, gaping at the girl behind Kurt. "Nan, it's her!" she added in a whisper.

Nancy couldn't believe how different Terry was in person. She was petite, barely five feet two. Instead of the glamorous outfits she wore on PTV, she had on loose khaki pants and a man's button-down shirt. Her jet-black hair was cut short and hung straight; her large violet eyes highlighted an already expressive face.

"I guess you know who I am," Terry said. She must have noticed Nancy checking out her clothes, because she said, "Not exactly high fashion, huh? Clothes for rehearsals aren't what I wear on PTV." Nancy immediately liked Terry's straightforwardness.

The man with them was in his late twenties, wearing a sports jacket, an open-necked shirt, and chinos. Of medium height, he had brown hair and dark slate blue eyes. He smiled when Terry linked her arm through his.

"This is Logan Chaffee, my friend and manager," Terry said.

As everyone took seats at Bess and Nancy's table, a waiter ran up to take orders. "Isn't Charleston the most beautiful place?" Terry exclaimed. "I wish I could explore it, but the show's had me on the run since I left New York."

"How are rehearsals going?" Nancy asked.

"Great," Kurt replied. "There are a few rough spots, of course, but we have a few days to work them out. We'll be fine, and this young lady"— he nodded at Terry—"is going to be fantastic."

Terry smiled happily. "Kurt is incredible. We'd all be lost without him. And no one writes better musicals than Stuart Firman, right, Logan?"

Logan nodded. "That's what they say."

Since it was just four-thirty, Bess and Nancy split an appetizer of barbecued ribs. The other three dug into whole dinners of seafood, hush puppies, and spicy cornbread that was a specialty at CJ's.

"We have to eat now," Terry explained, "because dress rehearsal starts in two hours. I hope we'll get to finish early tonight because I'm due on McCallum Island at ten tomorrow."

"McCallum?" Nancy echoed. "That tennis and golf resort just off the coast of Charleston? What's going on there?"

Terry's violet eyes sparkled. "My boyfriend. Pat's playing an exhibition match with a group of touring pros. I haven't seen him in two months!

We'll be celebrating our first year and a half together."

Nancy knew that Pat Flynn was one of the best professional tennis players in the world and knew that he and Terry were an item.

"It'll be great to see him," Terry added.

"I saw Pat on TV in a match last week," Bess said. "It was wild. He got mad at someone and started yelling and—" She stopped suddenly. "Oh, sorry, Terry."

Terry said, "Hey, you're not telling me anything new. I know Pat's got a temper."

"I'll say," Logan said. "What a jerk!"

"Logan." Nancy saw Terry give her manager a cool glance.

"I was just—" Logan began.

Terry cut him off. "You've said it a hundred times before. I don't need advice, Logan." The two of them sat glaring at each other.

Logan may be her friend, Nancy thought, but there's tension between them. Nancy changed the subject by saying to Kurt, "Bess and I are really excited about seeing the show from backstage."

"It gets crazy back there, but I think you'll enjoy it. Why don't you come to tonight's rehearsal? Be at the stage door of the Majestic Theater by six-fifteen."

* * *

"Warn lights seventy-eight . . . *go* lights seventy-eight. Stand by, sound thirty-four!"

The stage manager had been rattling off light and sound cues since the beginning of the rehearsal. Nancy and Bess didn't have a clue as to what the cues meant, but they saw that he was very busy, much too busy to talk to them.

The middle-aged man wore a headset over his thinning hair. He sat at a table behind the stage near where Nancy and Bess were standing. Kurt had introduced him as Tim Delevan.

Nancy admired Tim's ability to concentrate with all the quiet but frantic activity. Stagehands carrying props and set pieces scurried around him as curtains and backdrops were raised and lowered from up high. Figures scurried on catwalks above them, too. Nancy and Bess could hear singing and some lines from the stage, but the heavy curtains kept them from seeing the rehearsal. Still, Nancy decided that what was going on backstage had to be almost as interesting as the show itself.

Chorus members exited and raced by, almost stepping on Nancy's feet. Terry followed, breathing hard. She smiled at Nancy and Bess. "It's going great! Got to change!" she called out as she ran by.

"What's this?" Bess whispered a second later, picking something up. She held out a filmy cape that glittered with gold thread. "Terry must have dropped it. What if she needs it?"

Nancy saw that Tim was too busy to be disturbed. "I'll see if I can get this to her," she said.

She headed in the direction Terry had run and ended up in a dim corridor. Up ahead to the left was a door marked Dressing Rooms. Nancy started down the empty corridor. The only light came from a few low wattage bulbs in wall brackets.

Just before the dressing room door was another door, partly ajar. As Nancy went by, she heard a noise. "Terry?" she called, listening intently. No one answered. Then a voice rose in the beginning of a scream that was abruptly cut off. *Something was wrong!* Nancy's whole body tensed as she pushed open the door.

In the faint light she could just make out Terry's petite figure struggling with a taller form directly behind her. As Nancy's eyes adjusted to the dark, she gasped at what she saw. The other person had wrapped an arm around Terry's throat in a deadly stranglehold!

Chapter

Two

Nancy lunged forward. She had gone only a step when the assailant turned and stared at her through the eyeholes of a ski mask. Terry was shoved into Nancy, and the actress stumbled and knocked her off balance. Both girls fell to the floor. Seeing the attacker cut around her, Nancy reached out to grab at the person's leg, but the attacker brushed her off and ran.

Breathing hard, Nancy helped Terry to get up. "Are you okay?"

"I think so." Nancy saw no signs of injury, but Terry's shaky voice indicated how scared she was.

9

"What happened?" Nancy asked.

"This guy grabbed me and dragged me in here. It was . . ." Terry shuddered and fell silent.

"You're sure it was a man?"

Terry nodded. "I'm almost positive it was a guy. He said, 'Drop out of the show, or drop out of the world.' I was so scared . . ." She trailed off, and Nancy could see that she was on the verge of tears.

"Any idea who it was?" Nancy gently prodded.

"No." Terry took several deep breaths, trying to pull herself together. "I'd better run. I've got to change for my next scene."

"You sure you can go on with the rehearsal?" Nancy asked, worried.

"This is supposed to be a nonstop run-through. I can't *not* go on."

Impressed by the actress's grit, Nancy nodded. "Okay, but later talk to me about what happened."

"In my dressing room. I've got to go now!"

"Terry!" Nancy picked up the filmy gold cape, which had fallen to the floor. "You dropped this."

Terry took it and smiled. "Thanks," she said, and ducked through the door that led to the dressing rooms.

When Nancy rejoined her backstage, Bess asked, "Did you find Terry?" Her mouth fell open when Nancy told her what had happened. "Oh, no!" she gasped. "Who'd want to hurt Terry?"

"I don't know." Nancy lowered her voice as someone launched into a song onstage. "But after rehearsal, I'm going to find out."

Nancy and Bess knocked and went into Terry's dressing room, a small cubicle with a table and chair facing a mirror lit by bare bulbs. A worn armchair and couch completed the furniture. Sitting in a bathrobe in front of the mirror, Terry was wiping off her makeup. Kurt and Logan were there, too.

"You lost your concentration in the ballroom scene, but otherwise it went great," Kurt told her.

Terry continued to wipe at her face and stare grimly into the mirror.

"Ter, is something wrong?" Logan asked.

"You have to tell them, Terry," Nancy said. The actress nodded and described the backstage attack.

"I told you," Logan said, furious. "I *knew* it wasn't a harmless crank. He's physically attacked Terry now, and we have to do something!"

"Have other things happened?" Nancy asked, surprised.

Logan nodded. "I think we should bring the police in now."

11

"No!" Terry stood up abruptly, her violet eyes flashing. "I said *no police*. They'd be a distraction. They might even stop the opening. This show will open on schedule. I'm perfectly all right."

"Excuse my butting in," Bess said, "but Nan is a really good detective. Maybe she can help."

Nancy watched as Kurt and Logan exchanged a doubtful glance.

"Maybe she *can* help," Terry said, sitting down again.

"Okay," Nancy said, "let's run through exactly what's happened. It might help us figure out who's responsible."

Terry took a deep breath. "I've been getting unsigned nasty notes," she started. "The message is always, 'Quit the show or else.' I assumed they were harmless, the usual crank mail."

"When did they start?" Nancy asked.

"Just after we got to Charleston," Logan replied. "Four weeks ago."

"Can I look at them?" Nancy questioned.

"I threw most of them away," the manager replied. "There didn't seem to be much we could do about them," he explained.

Nancy frowned. "Were they mailed? Was there a postmark?"

"The first ones—about four or five—were mailed," Logan answered. "I open the fan mail, but unfortunately, I didn't think to look at the postmarks. The last two notes were left at the front desk of the hotel. I still have those."

"So the sender is here in Charleston," Bess put in.

"Yup," Logan said. "After all, he tried to strangle Terry tonight."

"Logan," Nancy said, "we can't be sure that the attacker is the same person who sent the notes." She turned to Terry. "Can you think of anyone who might want you out of the show?"

Kurt answered for the actress. "No one. Everyone loves Terry."

"Nancy, can you keep Terry company?" Kurt asked. "Watch her back, so to speak."

Nancy liked Terry, and she didn't want to see anything stop her from doing the show. "Sure. I'll do everything I can to help. I want to see the two notes you have. And if I feel the police have to be called in, then we call them in, okay?"

"Agreed," Terry said. "Now——"

Just then a young woman knocked once and entered the dressing room. She had a dancer's slender build, dark brown hair, and heavy make-up. "Hi," she said, perching on the arm of the chair next to Kurt. "Terry, you kind of messed up the ballroom scene, huh?"

"Thanks, Holly," Terry said icily. She turned to Nancy and Bess. "Meet Holly Bartell, my understudy. She always points out my mistakes."

"I'm only trying to help," Holly protested.

"We're in the middle of something, if you don't mind," Kurt said, not smiling.

"Well, excuse me." Holly got up and left.

"We can't let *her* hear about this," Terry said. "The only thing she'd like more than juicy gossip would be my part."

Nancy filed the information away. Holly obviously stood to gain if Terry quit the show. Where had Holly been when Terry was attacked? she wondered. "I'd like to go to McCallum Island with you tomorrow, Terry. Bess, too. Okay?"

"Sounds good," Terry said, stifling a yawn. "I'll bring the notes I've saved."

"You're supposed to meet Pat at McCallum's main lodge?" Bess asked.

It was early the next morning, and Bess, Terry, and Nancy were taking the forty-minute boat ride from Charleston's City Marina to the famous island resort. Leaning against the railing on the deck, Nancy gazed out at the gentle blue-gray water. Pelicans and sea gulls glided overhead, and a warm salty breeze ruffled her hair.

"That's right," Terry replied, smiling. "I can't wait to see him. Oh—here are the notes I told you about last night."

Nancy carefully examined the pieces of paper. Both notes were on lined yellow paper, in large block letters: OPENING NIGHT IS A LIFE-TIME AWAY! GET OUT! and WE CAN GET

YOU ANYTIME, ANYWHERE. QUIT THE SHOW.

Putting the notes away, Nancy looked at Terry and noticed the dark half-circles under the actress's eyes. She obviously hadn't slept well. "How are you feeling?" Nancy asked.

Terry smiled nervously. "I look like a mess, don't I? And I'm having this big reunion with my boyfriend. Oh, well. I'm okay, really."

Nancy had her doubts, but didn't want to worry Terry. She decided not to ask anything more about the notes for now.

Thirty minutes later the boat approached a sleek landing lined by palmetto trees, white sand beaches, and graceful sea grass. The wood and glass buildings were both sleek and "beachy." A colorful flag beside the dock bore the resort's logo—a stylized *M* with a palmetto tree on either side.

As the girls made their way up to the main lodge, they could see the tennis courts, pools, and part of a golf course.

Reporters and TV crews were all over the lobby, but in her sunglasses and floppy hat, Terry had gone unrecognized so far. The media was more interested in the tennis players.

Nancy was impressed by the sleek, low-slung couches and chairs that furnished the lobby. Through an arched doorway, she could see a fancy restaurant with an empty bandstand at one end. Huge windows framed a terrace and golf course outside.

As she took in the lobby, Nancy noticed a familiar-looking, tall, brown-haired guy. His back was to her, but when he turned she recognized him immediately. "Frank Hardy's here!" she exclaimed. "And there's Joe!"

Frank's handsome, seventeen-year-old brother had joined him. A year younger and an inch shorter than Frank, Joe had blond hair, blue eyes, and a rugged build. Nancy and Bess and the Hardys were good friends because the four of them had worked together on cases around the world.

"I don't believe it! Frank! Joe!" Bess called as she and Nancy waved energetically.

Joe saw them, dug an elbow into his brother's side, and waved back. The Hardys pushed through the crowd to greet Nancy and Bess with hugs.

"It's great to see you!" Nancy said. Lowering her voice, she asked, "Is this a vacation or a case?"

"A case," Frank replied. "What about you?"

"We came to have fun, but I guess we're on a case now, too." Nancy introduced Terry to Frank and Joe.

The Terry Alford, from PTV?" Joe asked. "I love your show. I watch it all the time!"

"Thanks," Terry said, her eyes searching the crowd, no doubt looking for Pat.

"Terry, you date Pat Flynn, right? Is that why you're here?" Frank asked thoughtfully.

"That's right," she answered distractedly.

"Fantastic," Frank said, but Nancy noticed that the thoughtful expression remained on his face. "Er, can Joe and I see you alone for a minute, Nan?"

"Sure," Nancy told him, wondering what was up. The Hardys led Nancy outside to an area dotted with tables and chairs. "What's up?" she asked.

"I don't want to scare Terry, but the guy running this tour asked Joe and me to protect Pat. It seems somebody has it in for him. There've been a couple of incidents."

"Tell me about them," Nancy said eagerly.

"This tour of exhibition matches started ten days ago," said Joe. "Consolidated Motors is the sponsor. Well, anyway, Pat's problems first started out as stupid pranks. Some pizzas that he never ordered were delivered to his room. Then he started getting late-night phone calls. At first they'd just hang up, but then they started making threats."

Frank went on. "Three days ago a cherry bomb was thrown at Pat during one of his matches. It was big enough to make a crater in the clay court,

17

not to mention that Pat could have been seriously burned. That was when Butch Van Voort, the guy in charge of the tour, called us in to help."

"Any progress?" asked Nancy.

"None," Joe said, rolling his eyes. "So, tell us about your case."

After Nancy told the brothers about Terry's problems, Joe said, "She isn't backing down, huh? She must be one tough lady. Who—"

"Nan!" Bess ran out and interrupted them. Nancy knew even before Bess told her that Pat had arrived. All the reporters had rushed to the lobby entrance and surrounded the young tennis star.

Pat burst through the crowd and ran up to Terry, his arms open wide. "Hey, Terry, babe!" Terry slipped into his arms and they embraced.

Nancy had never seen Pat Flynn in person. On TV he seemed small and wiry, but now she saw that he was six feet tall. His strength was obvious even through his white and aqua warm-up suit. His curly blond hair was bleached almost white by the sun.

The reporters closed in once again and jostled Nancy aside. Strobe lights flashed, floodlights glared, and questions were fired at the couple. Pat grinned broadly, and Nancy could tell that he enjoyed all the attention.

Holding up his hands, he laughed. "Slow down! I can only answer one question at a time."

Casually he lowered an arm and draped it around Terry's shoulders.

"Hey!" Bess yelled as a photographer elbowed her, getting in position for a picture. Nancy found the frenzy of the media a little rough. Everyone was shouting and shoving, jockeying for position. Hands thrust microphones forward and held up too bright lights for the TV cameras.

As she was trying to take it all in, Nancy saw a gloved hand thrust out from between two shouting reporters. She froze when she saw what the hand held. It was a pistol! The large-caliber automatic was capped with a bulbous silencer and was pointed directly at Pat's chest!

Nancy tried to move, but the reporters had her trapped. Before she could even open her mouth to shout a warning, the gloved hand squeezed the trigger. There was a barely audible noise.

Phffft.

For Nancy, time froze. The gloved hand pulled back and vanished as Nancy watched a bright red stain spread across Pat's gleaming white jacket.

Chapter
Three

$\mathbf{F}$RANK LEAPT to Pat's side, staring in shock at the crimson blotch on the tennis player's jacket. "Joe, he's been hit!" he called out as he eased Pat to the floor. "Try to find the shooter!"

"Pat! Pat!" Terry screamed, kneeling beside him. Her face went completely white. "Quick, someone *do* something!"

Nancy and Bess tried to block the crowd from Pat, who was clutching at his chest.

"How bad is it?" Frank asked, kneeling beside him. Some protection he and Joe had provided —their client had gotten shot with them standing right next to him!

Pat blinked, then blinked again, obviously confused. "I—I don't feel anything. What happened?"

What's going on here? Frank wondered. Pat didn't seem as if he was in any pain. Frank dabbed the red stain with his finger and sniffed.

"It's not blood," he said. "It's some kind of a dye. Relax, everybody, no one's hurt."

The journalists couldn't hear Frank and continued shoving, elbowing, and shouting into microphones. Frank looked up and saw Joe's head over the crowd. Joe shook his head, indicating he'd had no luck. He tried to ask his brother something, but couldn't make himself heard.

"EVERYONE, SHUT UP!" he finally roared. Abruptly, the lobby quieted. "Pat, are you okay?"

The tennis player was still dazed, but he nodded and got to his feet. "Yeah, except for being scared to death."

"Let's look around," Frank suggested to Joe and Nancy. He hated leaving Pat and Terry to face the reporters alone, but finding the shooter was his top priority.

Frank, Joe, Nancy, and Bess spread out to check for anyone or anything suspicious. As Frank walked past a wooden tub holding a broadleafed plant, something shiny caught his eye. In the tub lay a gleaming pistol. "Hey! I think I've found the weapon," he shouted.

The others ran over, along with several reporters. Frank knelt down to examine the pistol.

"Maybe we shouldn't touch it," Bess objected. "I mean, what about fingerprints?"

"There won't be fingerprints," Nancy pointed out. "The shooter wore a glove."

"And you can't do ballistic tests on a water gun," Frank added, picking it up. It was a very realistic-looking toy. When he pulled the trigger, a jet of red liquid splashed into the planter.

Pat and Terry had broken away from the crowd, and when Frank looked up he saw a man walk directly into their path, blocking their escape.

"Yo, Flynn! I guess you'll do anything to get your face on TV, huh?"

"Not me, Lassiter." Pat glared angrily. "That was a stupid prank, the kind of garbage *you* would pull. Where were you five minutes ago, anyway?"

"That's none of your business," he responded as the reporters closed in once again.

"Maybe I'll make it my business." Pat's hands were clenched and his jaw tight.

"That's Alan Lassiter, Pat's main tennis rival," Frank whispered to Nancy. "He's a year older than Pat, twenty-three, and they have a long history of fighting with each other."

Nancy eyed Lassiter. He was a gangly six feet

four, lean and wiry. He had brown hair, brown eyes, and a sarcastic expression.

Several cameras clicked as Terry grabbed Pat's arm.

"Cut it out!" roared an angry voice. Nancy turned and watched an older man shoulder his way through the reporters. He slipped in between the athletes and said, "Save it for your match."

Nancy breathed a sigh of relief as Pat and Alan stepped apart. Just then an exquisitely dressed red-haired woman in her midtwenties strode rapidly into the lobby. She was waving a sheaf of papers.

"Get your press kits here!" she called, drawing the journalists away from Pat and Alan. "You won't blow this horseplay out of proportion, will you?" She skillfully maneuvered the reporters farther away from Pat and Alan.

"This isn't over, hotshot," Alan hissed before stalking off.

"Sorry, Butch," Pat told the older man. "But he—"

"I don't want to hear it!" the man snapped. "You and Alan are supposed to be adults and professionals. You'd better act accordingly!"

Pat's jaw tightened again. "Some clown just scared me to death. I don't need more grief from you!"

The older, gray-haired man sighed. "Okay, Pat. Sorry, but I can't have public brawls."

Pat nodded. "You're right. I'll try to cool it with Alan from now on." He took Terry's hand and drew her forward. "Butch, this is my girlfriend, Terry Alford. Terry, meet Butch Van Voort, head honcho of these exhibition matches."

"Hello," Terry said, and introduced Nancy and Bess.

"Hi," Butch said, and smiled, his tan face crinkling into a network of fine wrinkles around his eyes and mouth. Nancy remembered reading that he had been a tennis pro a few years earlier.

Pat mumbled, "See you," to everyone as he and Terry walked away.

Butch turned to the Hardys. "What happened?" he asked.

Frank told him about the water pistol incident. Butch chewed his lower lip and said, "I can't have any more bad publicity—Consolidated might pull their backing. Have you got any leads?"

"Sorry." Joe shook his head. "It's only been a couple of days. All we know is Pat has enemies on this tour."

Butch frowned. "That's not news. Pat is our big draw. People either love him or hate him, but they pay to see him. I need him at his best for the rest of the tour."

"We're doing what we can," Frank said.

"I hope it's good enough." With that, Butch walked away.

"Tough case," Nancy said sympathetically.

"That's for sure," Joe agreed. "Pat has lots of enemies. Besides Lassiter there's Gunnar Hedstrom."

"Who's he?" Bess asked.

"Alan's coach and trainer," Frank explained. "He benefits if Alan gets top ranking. Also, Gunnar coached Pat until last year, when Pat dumped him. Pat isn't exactly complimentary when he talks about Gunnar's talent and personality."

"Speak of the devil," Joe said, pointing to the lobby entrance.

The man who was approaching was in his thirties, Nancy saw. He had a droopy mustache and long brown hair held in place by a red headband.

"Where's Alan?" Gunnar asked in a slight accent.

"He just left," Frank replied. "Did you hear what happened to Pat just now?"

Nancy thought she saw a slight grin under Gunnar's mustache. "I heard. What is that saying? 'What goes around, comes around.' See you later," he said. He walked to the other side of the lobby, where the red-haired woman was waving goodbye to the last few reporters.

"He won't lose sleep over Pat's problems," Joe said to Nancy and Bess.

"Frank! Joe! I want to talk to you!"

The red-haired woman was hailing them from the front desk. "Butch just told me about the water pistol business. I guess I arrived in time to stop a public relations disaster. Our sponsor, Consolidated Motors, would have *loved* that. Where were *you* at the time?"

Nancy saw Joe redden as Frank spoke up. "We were next to Pat, on the job."

The woman coolly studied Nancy and Bess. "Are you press?"

"No, just friends of ours," Frank said. "Nancy Drew and Bess Marvin, meet Kitty Wills, the tour publicist."

Kitty waved them off and went back to talking to Frank and Joe. "From now on try to get with the program and protect Pat, will you?"

Nancy saw that Joe was about to explode, so Frank answered for them. "Okay, we'll get to the bottom of this," he said.

"I'll believe that when I see it," Kitty said, and whirled around and stalked off.

"What does she want from you, anyway?" Bess demanded. "What a witch!"

"She does seem unreasonable," Nancy agreed.

Frank shrugged. "Kitty's under pressure, and she's right—we haven't done much so far."

"You've just started, though," Bess said. She

turned to Joe. "Oh, what about a little game of tennis tomorrow? Terry's coming back over here to watch Pat's match. So we'll have to come, too. Shall we play before the match?"

Nancy hoped her mouth wasn't hanging open. What was this? Bess was actually suggesting physical activity. Then Nancy saw the bright smile Bess shot Joe. Even though they were just good friends, Bess and Joe had always enjoyed flirting. Obviously, Bess didn't mind playing tennis—as long as it was with Joe.

"Let's say ten o'clock?" Bess said. "We have to get back to Charleston now. Terry has to rehearse."

Joe shielded his eyes from the sun while he and Frank watched Pat practice. For the past hour the brothers had been going over the case, but hadn't come up with much.

"Can you see Alan pulling these pranks?" Joe asked.

Frank shrugged and thought out loud. "He hates Pat, and he does stand to gain a lot if he gets that number-one ranking."

"But he'd lose a lot if he got caught," Joe pointed out. "Would it be worth the risk?"

"Don't ask me," Frank replied, holding up his hands.

Joe gave an impressed nod as Pat hit a sizzling backhand down the line. The other guy never got near the ball. "That's it for me," Pat called to his opponent. "Good session."

Getting up from the stands, Joe and Frank fell in step with Pat, walking him to the condos where all the pros were staying, across a courtyard from the main lodge.

"I know Lassiter had something to do with the water pistol," said Pat as they went inside. "Him or Gunnar, or both of them maybe."

He unlocked his door and moved into his room. "I don't trust those two. They—"

Pat froze just inside the door.

"Pat? What is it?" Joe asked.

Pat said nothing. An alarm went off in Joe's head, and he pushed by Pat.

The living room was a shambles. Torn clothing and equipment were scattered everywhere. Every surface in the room was covered with debris, except one chair. There, a single object caught Joe's eye.

In the middle of the chair lay a male doll, dressed in tennis whites. It had been pinned to the upholstery by a long, gleaming knife through its chest.

Chapter
Four

Tʜᴀᴛ's ᴍʏ good-luck charm!" Pat shouted. He pushed past Frank and Joe, removed the knife, picked up the doll, then threw it down again. "I've had it with Alan and Gunnar!"

Frank grabbed Pat's arm. "Chill out, Pat. We don't know who—"

"It was Alan and Gunnar, I tell you!" Pat screamed.

While Frank tried to calm Pat down, Joe began searching the room. "This door's been jimmied," Joe said, standing by the glass doors leading to the balcony.

"Let go of me," Pat growled through clenched jaws. "It's payback time."

Frank stood his ground. "No way, Pat."

"If you fight, it'll make the news, and that'll only hurt the tournament," Joe added.

"But it'll make me feel a lot better." Joe was relieved to see that Pat's white-hot anger was already cooling. Pat sagged into a chair, tossing aside a shredded sweatshirt.

"How long have you had that doll?" Joe asked.

"Two years. I bring it to every match."

"So people know about it?" Frank asked.

"Sure. Most of the players kid me about it."

"We'd better talk to Alan and Gunnar about this," Frank said.

Pat gave the Hardys a sullen nod, then started sifting through his wrecked things.

Before leaving, the Hardys searched the condo thoroughly for any clue as to the identity of the attacker. They came up empty-handed.

"He really seemed upset," Frank said, once they were in the hall.

"He did calm down, but I still think he might do something crazy. We've got to figure out who's behind this, and fast. He said his place was okay after lunch, so it must have happened between about one-thirty and now"—he checked his watch—"three o'clock. We need to know who was around here then."

"Let's check out the tennis courts. We have to find Gunnar and Alan," said Frank.

The Hardys found Alan and Gunnar at the courts reserved for the tour pros. They were working on Alan's serve.

"That's a mean serve you've got," said Joe, amazed by the whiplike motion of Alan's long arm that gave the ball its speed.

Alan smiled thinly, but didn't reply.

"We're busy," Gunnar said. "What do you want?"

"You must put in a lot of practice time," Frank observed. "I mean, you've been here—what, an hour? Two?"

Joe stood back and listened. When it came to being diplomatic, Frank was definitely the guy for the job. Joe just hoped his brother got the answers they needed.

Alan's smile became a sneer. "What's it to you, huh? Take a hike."

"I was only wondering—" Frank started, watching Alan toss the ball high.

Whap!

Alan's overhand smash hummed past Frank, inches from his head. Joe started forward angrily, but Frank caught his arm and smiled at Alan. "I won't ask for your autograph, after all. Let's go, Joe."

Joe scowled. "Well, *that* did a lot of good. We know exactly what we did before. Nothing."

Nancy and Bess were in Terry's dressing room at the theater, waiting while Terry got into her costume.

Nancy turned casually to Terry to ask about her relationship with Logan. No one was above suspicion. "How long has Logan been your manager?"

"Forever," Terry said, laughing. "He was my manager before I had a career to manage. On 'Home with the Hendersons,' Logan played my big brother. Backstage he helped me with my lines and homework, like a big brother. When he got older, he couldn't get acting work, so he went into the army."

"But you guys remained friends?" Bess asked.

"He got in touch again after he left the service. I had gotten too old for the 'Hendersons' and was out of work and depressed. He cheered me up and said something would come along. A little later he saw a trade paper item that PTV was looking for talent. He set up an audition for me," Terry explained. "When I got the job, I told him, 'You're my manager.' Simple as that."

"I sense there's tension between you, though," Nancy said.

Terry sighed. "Is it that obvious?"

Nancy quickly added, "If you'd rather not discuss it . . ."

"I see *Beauty* as a chance for a big move back into what I consider real acting, but Logan disagrees. He says I gave up a sure thing for a risky gamble."

"What's his problem with Pat?" Bess asked.

Terry shook her head unhappily. "They just don't get along. Logan thinks Pat's not good enough for me. He still wants to be my big brother, but I don't need one anymore."

Nancy nodded sympathetically. "What about your understudy?" Nancy had guessed Holly didn't like Terry very much.

Terry didn't seem to have heard Nancy. "Whoops, almost forgot!" She snapped her fingers and jumped up. "I have to get my notes on last night's run-through. Come on."

Terry led the girls backstage to find Tim Delevan and get her notes. Tim was checking lights out front, in the auditorium, so the three trooped down the stairs and up the center aisle for Terry's notes.

Turning to leave, they saw a pretty girl about Nancy and Bess's age, wearing patched overalls and a T-shirt, enter the house. Her dark lipstick was heavy and almost matched her dark metallic red hair.

"Hey, Terry!" the girl called. "How you doing?"

"Fine, Leese," Terry said. "Meet my friends, Nancy Drew and Bess Marvin. This is Leese Tolliver."

"Pleased to meet you," the girl said with a sunny smile.

"Are you in the show?" Nancy asked.

Leese shook her head. "What's Leese short for?" Bess asked.

"For Felicia." Leese's nose wrinkled in distaste. "My grandparents are the only ones who use it. They're into formal names and stuff. They raised me after my parents died. Beaufort and Andrea Tolliver. Ever hear of them?"

"No," said Bess.

"They're heavyweights around Charleston," Leese explained. "Grandpa ran Southern EXPOsure till the city decided to liven it up. He was real unhappy about that."

Terry put an arm around Leese's shoulders. "Leese is dating one of the guys in our band."

Leese nodded enthusiastically. "Cal Lipton. He's an awesome guitarist. You can't *imagine* how upset Grandpa and Grandma are, though. But I try not to care. I like Cal, and I love rock. Isn't *Beauty and the Beat* fantastic?"

Nancy smiled. She liked Leese's openness and friendliness. "We've only heard it from the wings."

"How do you like Charleston? Have you been over by Shem Creek yet?"

"Not yet," Nancy said. "But we love everything we've seen so far."

"Well, you should definitely check out Shem Creek. It's where the fishing and crabbing boats are. It's so *funky!* And the restaurants—say, do you like seafood?"

Bess's eyes lit up. "Love it!"

"Then have dinner with me! I'm meeting my grandparents at The Crab Pot at seven. Cal and Terry will be working late, so I'd love the company. With you there, Grandpa and Grandma won't be able to yell about the company I keep. How about it?"

Just then Kurt Zimmer and another man came through the auditorium door and headed for the girls. He hugged Terry and asked, "You got your notes? Any questions?"

When Terry shook her head, Kurt said, "Okay. You ready to rehearse?"

"I'm ready," Terry said. She turned to Nancy and Bess. "Go ahead with Leese. It'll be good fun and great food. We're going to be starting and stopping this afternoon to work on sound cues, so it'll be pretty boring. You should check out the EXPO."

Nancy wasn't sure she should leave Terry alone all that time, but the actress said, "Go. I'll be fine, really."

"Okay," Nancy replied. "But we'll come back to check on you right after dinner."

"Before you leave," Kurt said, "Nancy and Bess, meet Stuart Firman. He wrote *Beauty and the Beat* and about eight other hit shows. Or is it nine?"

"Nine," Stuart replied, smiling. He looked as if he was just past thirty. His dark hair was short and he wore rimless glasses.

"I love your work," Nancy told him.

"And I appreciate your help, Nancy. Terry's very important to us," Stuart said.

Nancy turned to Leese. "How do we get to The Crab Pot?"

Leese gave them directions. "Don't dress up, and *do* bring your appetites! I'll meet you there at seven, okay?"

"Fine." Nancy turned to Bess. "Come on, let's check out the EXPO for a few hours. There are special events all over Charleston."

"Cool! There's a bluegrass band set up in the Battery," Bess said, skimming one of her glossy EXPO pamphlets. "It's at the tip of the city."

The girls walked down King Street, one of the city's main drags. On the way they saw mime performers, face painters, and booths where people sold all kinds of clothes and crafts. Before long, Nancy could hear lively strains of bluegrass music.

King Street had come to an end at a park with a band set up in a gazebo there. On the far side of the park, a stone wall marked the edge of the city. The blue water of Charleston Harbor sparkled beyond.

Nancy couldn't help tapping her feet to the music. "I don't know about you," she said, grinning at Bess, "but I'm ready to dance. Let's go!"

The Crab Pot was definitely funky, Nancy thought a few hours later. It was a ramshackle building on an inlet that led to open water. The docks were lined with fishing boats.

Leese met them in front of the restaurant, still in the same overalls and T-shirt she'd been wearing earlier.

"It's buffet night," Leese told them as they went inside, raising her voice over the noise. A long buffet table filled the restaurant's front room. Through an open doorway, Nancy saw another room filled with simple wooden tables and booths. "Get in line and I'll find Grandpa and Grandma. Try the she-crab soup. It's a local specialty!"

Nancy and Bess went to the end of the long line at the buffet. People moved on either side of the table. Nancy's stomach growled when she saw the steaming kettles of soup, pots of crayfish and crabs, and trays of grilled snapper, halibut, and other ocean fish. As Nancy waited, she heard a voice filter through the noise, "Never wanted *Beauty and the Beat* here. It attracts a bad element."

Instantly alert, Nancy turned toward the voice. It was from a man across from her. He was about sixty, tall and elegantly dressed in a linen suit and paisley tie. His gray hair was silvery at the temples. The man he spoke to was short and middle-aged, with a sour expression, horn-rimmed glasses, and a tweed jacket over a black turtleneck.

The short man nodded. "Absolutely. It's pure trash. I'd love to see it shut down."

Could these two be involved in the attack on Terry? Nancy wondered. The first man smiled and glanced around furtively. Nancy quickly turned her head, so he wouldn't realize she had been listening. She heard his next words clearly, though.

"Shut down the show? I think that can be arranged."

Chapter

Five

NANCY'S MIND RACED. Who are they? And why do they want to shut down *Beauty and the Beat?*

Nancy nudged Bess. "You see the two men across from us? The one in the white suit and his friend?" she whispered.

"Sure. What about them?" Bess asked, dishing up some shrimp.

In a low voice, Nancy told her friend what she'd overheard. "We've got to keep an eye on them, Bess, so move a little faster," Nancy said. They hurried to fill their plates, coming to the end of their line a few seconds after the two men.

They started to follow them into the large dining room, but a party of about ten stepped in front of them, blocking their way. Once they'd passed, Bess asked, "Do you see them?"

"No, but they're here, somewhere. We'll—"

"Nan! Bess!" Leese made her way toward them from between the crowded tables. "Come on! My grandparents are here."

Nancy was frustrated. She had to find out who those men were before they left!

"Come on." Leese urged them to follow her.

Nancy and Bess had no choice but to follow.

"Here we are," Leese announced, leading Nancy and Bess to an alcove. There, sitting at a table, was a woman in her late fifties in an elegant green silk dress—and the two men who had been talking about shutting down the show!

"Nancy Drew, Bess Marvin," said Leese, "meet my grandparents, Beaufort and Andrea Tolliver. And this is, uh—"

"Warren Brophy, the playwright," Beau supplied, dipping his head in a bow. "Please sit. Welcome to Charleston."

Why would Leese's grandfather want to ruin the show? Nancy wondered. Then she realized that Mr. Tolliver was asking her a question. "I'm sorry, I didn't hear you," she said, smiling.

"Do you like our city?" Beau repeated.

"Oh, yes," Nancy replied. "It's lovely."

Leese's grandfather beamed proudly.

"Definitely," Bess echoed Nancy. "And Southern EXPOsure is great, too."

Andrea sighed and frowned. "It *was,* when Beau was in charge, but standards have declined."

"Now, Andrea," Beau said, taking her hand. "Young people have different tastes."

Andrea sniffed. "I don't understand those tastes. That loud, raucous music . . ."

Leese rolled her eyes at Nancy and stood up. "I'm going to get some dinner. Be right back."

Beau stared sadly after his granddaughter as she walked away. Then he focused on Nancy. "Will you girls be in Charleston long?"

"For a week," Nancy replied.

"Then you must come to our lawn party," Andrea said, smiling. "It's in three days. If you like formal gardens, ours are unusually fine."

"Sounds like fun," Bess replied. Nancy nodded her agreement. Maybe they'd have a chance to check out Beau Tolliver and his plans for *Beauty and the Beat* at the party.

"Excellent," said Beau. "How nice to meet sensible young people."

"You're a playwright, Mr. Brophy," Nancy said to the shorter man. "Is a play of yours being performed here?"

Brophy smirked. "No, the people who attend the EXPO prefer amplified noise and screeching."

"If I still ran the festival, a play of Warren's would be a major event," Beau added. "But I've got no say. Warren is involved in the EXPO. He's writing an article contrasting Charleston's beauty with the uglier elements of the EXPO."

Nancy exchanged a quick look with Bess. "Like *Beauty and the Beat?*" Nancy asked, trying to shift the conversation to that subject.

"Precisely," Brophy answered. "Stuart Firman's latest monstrosity."

Bess dropped a crayfish shell on a growing pile on her plate. "You're not a fan of his?"

"Hardly." Brophy scowled. "Glitz and noise have replaced ideas and style in the theater, and no one is more to blame than Stuart Firman."

Nancy noted that Brophy's voice was venomous when he mentioned Stuart. "Have you had plays performed here?" she asked.

Brophy shook his head. "I had hoped to open my latest at the EXPO, but when Beau was replaced by a trendy hustler, I got a form letter saying, 'Thanks, but no thanks.'"

"Where did you meet Felicia?" Andrea asked Nancy and Bess.

"At the theater," Nancy replied without thinking.

"The theater!" Beau exclaimed, his expression darkening. "So she was with that scruffy musician."

"His name is Cal," said Leese, approaching the

table. "He's *not* scruffy, and he happens to have studied music in a conservatory." She sat down next to Nancy with a plateful of crabs, one of which she grabbed and started to pull apart.

Andrea winced and said, "Felicia, where are your manners?"

Nancy decided that now was not the time to ask Beau why he was no longer running the EXPO. Instead she talked about how lovely Charleston was. After what seemed like hours, she and Bess finally rose to go.

"I'll walk you out," said Leese after the girls had said goodbye to the Tollivers and Warren Brophy.

Outside, Nancy heard boats creaking and rubbing against docks. The air was balmy, with a smell of fish.

"Pretty grim, huh?" Leese said. "Welcome to my life."

"Your grandparents *are* a little old-fashioned," Nancy said. "But, anyway, the food was fabulous." Getting back to the case, she asked, "When was your grandfather replaced as director of the EXPO?"

"The board of directors voted him out six months ago," Leese answered. "He was mad enough to chew furniture."

"He doesn't seem the type," Bess commented.

"Don't kid yourself," Leese said. "He has a hot temper. *I* ought to know."

Nancy asked, "Has he known Warren Brophy long?"

"They wrote to each other when Grandpa ran EXPO," Leese answered. "Brophy looked him up when he got here two weeks ago, and they've been hanging out ever since, agreeing about how awful everything new is. By the way, you're not seriously thinking of going to their lawn party?"

"Actually, we were," Nancy said.

"I've got a better idea," Leese said. "My friends and I are having a barbecue at a park that day. It'll be great—ribs and fixings and good folks instead of stuffed shirts and fossils. Believe me, you'd rather be there. Bring Terry, too."

"We will, if we can," Nancy said as she and Bess climbed into their rented car.

As they drove back to the theater, Nancy and Bess reviewed the case.

"Do you think Beau Tolliver and Warren Brophy are connected with what's been happening to Terry?" Bess asked.

"Maybe," Nancy replied. "But if Terry leaves, her understudy, Holly Bartell, would step in. The show wouldn't close, and it could still be a hit."

A few minutes later they pulled into the Majestic Theater's parking lot. At the stage door, the doorman let them in. "You're in time for the last song. Rehearsal's going well," he said. "Go watch from the house."

The girls had learned that "the house" was

where the audience sat. They watched as the chorus performed a fast-moving song. Kurt made them run through it five times. Finally he called out, "Okay! Five-minute break."

Kurt and Stuart were sitting in the front row behind a table that was lit by a goose-neck lamp. Kurt scribbled notes as he and Stuart whispered back and forth. Nancy and Bess headed down to them.

Picking up an electric bullhorn, Kurt said, "While the chorus breaks, let's run Beauty's dream sequence, to make sure the effects are right. Let me know when you're ready, Tim."

Nancy watched as a lavish-looking backdrop of a palace was lowered. Eerie music sounded, and Terry appeared from behind the gauzy fabric door of the palace.

Nancy and Bess settled into two chairs to get their first real glimpse of the show. Terry looked beautiful, Nancy thought, and she projected a dreamlike quality.

Then without warning the entire theater was plunged into darkness and the music was cut off.

Nancy felt herself tense up as Bess clutched her arm. "What's going on?" someone called from the stage.

From the pitch blackness Nancy heard a shrill scream of fear. "No! NO!"

Goose bumps popped out on Nancy's arms. It was Terry!

Chapter

Six

SOMEONE HAD TERRY! Nancy groped for the penlight in her purse, snapped it on, and ran toward the stage.

Kurt's voice blared over the bullhorn. "Terry? Terry?" There was no answer. "Everyone, stay put!" he ordered. "Tim, give me work lights! Terry, are you okay? Talk to me!"

As Nancy reached the temporary stairs over the orchestra pit to the stage, Terry finally spoke.

"I'm all right." Her voice sounded quavery and frightened.

Just then the work lights blinked on, and pale

light filled the theater. Nancy gasped when she saw Terry hunched over on the floor. She reached Terry just as the crew members, led by Tim and Logan, came from the wings. Nancy helped the girl up while Logan got a chair for her. Terry sank into it, staring with unfocused eyes.

"Are you okay?" Nancy asked, kneeling beside her.

Terry nodded her head in quick jerks.

"What happened?" Bess asked quietly.

"When the lights went out, I froze. I mean, I didn't want to trip over anything. Then I *felt* someone by me, real close. A voice in my ear said, 'Your next role will be a corpse. You've been warned.' Then something cold and clammy touched my face. That's when I screamed."

Nancy turned to the stage manager. "Who was near the stage during that last number?"

"I don't remember," Tim answered. "I was too busy with cues to see exactly who was around."

"We were all busy," a burly crew member spoke up. "I didn't see anybody around who didn't belong."

Nancy nodded, then turned to Kurt.

He understood what she wanted and clapped his hands. "Listen up. Let's check the wiring. Some of the rest of you," he added, "check for intruders. If you see anyone or anything suspicious, give a yell. Let's move it!"

A dozen people began a search. Nancy and Bess stayed with Terry. "Did the voice sound even vaguely familiar?" Nancy asked the actress.

"No. It was very soft and scary."

"Did it sound like the voice of the person who attacked you backstage?" Nancy asked.

"I couldn't tell," Terry whispered miserably.

Nancy decided the person had to have been working with someone else. Otherwise, the attack couldn't have been timed to occur when the lights and sound went out.

Nancy's thoughts were interrupted as Kurt called out, "Nancy, Bess. Over here."

The two girls hurried over to where Tim and Kurt stood by an open metal door in the side wall of the stage. Several thick cables with plastic insulation fed into massive junction boxes. Nancy's mouth tightened into a grim line when she saw that the insulation from two cables had been peeled away, and a metal rod had been placed to connect the bare wires. There was a strong burning smell.

"All our wiring goes through here—lights and sound," Tim said. "Someone peeled away the insulation, made contact between these cables, and—*zzzt!*—everything shorted out."

"But there are lights now," Bess observed.

"The work lights are on an outside circuit," Tim explained. "Like an emergency line."

Nancy noticed some scratches near the

deadbolt on the metal door. "The lock was tampered with," she said. "Tim, you're sure you didn't see anyone near here just before the lights went out?"

The stage manager shrugged. "Sorry. I didn't notice anyone."

"This means the culprit must know the play and the setup of the theater," Nancy said as they walked back to Terry.

The crew members had returned to the stage. "Find anyone?" Kurt asked Logan, who had gone with them. "Anything suspicious?"

"No," Logan replied, standing beside Terry's chair. "Terry, I'm worried about you. Is performing in this show really worth your life?"

Terry took a deep breath and blinked back tears. When she spoke, though, her voice was steady. "I'm not going to let some maniac run my life. I'm standing by my decision. Will you stand by me?"

Logan's face reddened. "Haven't I always?"

"Terry!" Nancy saw Terry flinch as her name was shouted out from the wings. "Are you all right?" Holly Bartell ran onstage and went straight to Kurt. "If she wants time off, I'm ready to fill in. I mean, Terry will need to get herself together." Her tone was earnest, but Nancy thought she was overdoing it a little.

"Maybe Holly has a point," Kurt suggested.

"No!" Terry's jaw was clenched. "I'll be fine."

"But . . ." Holly protested. The understudy's desperation to do the role was obvious. Would she go so far as to attack Terry? Nancy wondered.

Terry confronted Holly, eyes flashing. "Thanks for your concern, but I'm fine!"

"Terry, go home and get some rest," Kurt said, moving smoothly between the actresses.

"Terry, Bess and I can stay with you tonight, if you want," Nancy offered.

Terry smiled gratefully. "Would you?"

"Absolutely," Bess chimed in. "Now I'll be able to say I stayed in a VIP suite."

By eleven P.M. Nancy and Bess had moved into Terry's elegant suite. The suite had a bedroom and a living room that were each larger and fancier than the room Nancy and Bess shared. The hotel had provided foldaway beds, which were set up in the living room.

Nancy answered a knock at the door, and Stuart Firman and Logan entered. Logan was carrying a dozen roses. "These are for you, Ter," he said.

"Thanks, Logan," she said, giving him a quick hug.

"We wanted to check on you," Stuart said.

"I'm okay, just tired," said Terry, yawning. "Night, all." She went into the bedroom and shut the door.

"Can you stick around and talk?" Nancy asked the two guys. They nodded.

"I need some background information," Nancy said. "For one thing, I need to know how Terry's doing in the show."

"How will that help you solve the case?" Logan asked, frowning.

Nancy wasn't sure, but her instincts told her she needed to know everything about the show if she was going to crack this case. "Humor me," she urged.

Logan nodded. "Well, between us, her voice isn't great. I was against her doing this show because if she flops she might not get another shot at acting so easily. You know she did an album?"

Nancy was startled. "No, I didn't."

"Last year. It was a bomb. We buried it fast, so it didn't hurt her," Logan explained. "But bombing in *Beauty* could wreck her new career. She left her job at PTV, so there's no going back."

"True, her voice is so-so," Stuart added. "Terry may not be a great singer, but she's a great *performer*. I know she'll come through on opening night."

"How would it affect the show if she dropped out?" Bess wanted to know.

"It would hurt us badly," Stuart replied. "Holly's good, but she's unknown. Terry's name will draw people. We need her."

"Terry and Holly don't seem to get along," Bess said.

Good going, Nancy silently cheered her friend.

Stuart smiled. "Holly thinks doing *Beauty* will make her a star. She's very hungry."

"Would you say she's desperate enough to try to force Terry to leave?" asked Nancy.

"Holly? No way," Stuart answered. "Sure, she's ambitious, but I don't think she'd know how to sabotage the theater wiring."

"She could be working with an accomplice," Nancy said, thinking aloud. "Tell me what you know about Warren Brophy," she said, changing the subject.

"Brophy?" Stuart gave her a puzzled glance.

Nancy nodded. "We met him tonight. He doesn't like you much."

Stuart snorted. "He *hates* me. My show won out over his for EXPO. He can't get over that."

"Would he resort to sabotage?" Nancy asked.

"He attacks me in his articles, and he's rude whenever he sees me," Stuart replied, frowning. "I wouldn't put it past him."

Logan's eyes narrowed. "You mean *he* could be mixed up in these threats against Terry?"

Nancy recalled Brophy's outburst at the restaurant. "It's a definite possibility."

Early the next morning Terry, Nancy, and Bess were back on the boat to McCallum Island.

"Do you play tennis?" Bess asked Terry.

"No, but believe me, I hear about it all the time," she answered. "Mostly I just watch Pat play on TV." Terry gazed out at the water. "We see each other so little. Our schedules don't let us get together often, and then it's usually just for a couple of days. Even when we're in the same city, it's hard to find time to spend together.

"Pat saw a lot of his last girlfriend, but they had other problems," Terry added. "Her temper is almost as bad as his."

"Is she a tennis player?" Bess asked.

"She's a publicist—that red-haired woman you said yelled at your friends yesterday after that water pistol incident," Terry said. "Kitty Wills.

"Well, she worked for Pat's agent as a publicist. When he dropped her for me, Kitty was furious. She quit his agent and started her own PR agency."

Terry made a wry face and added, "When Pat heard that Butch had hired Kitty, he hit the roof. But Butch said she was the best and refused to fire her. I just hope she and Pat don't have screaming matches like they did when Pat broke up with her."

" 'Screaming matches'?" Nancy echoed, making a mental note to tell the Hardys. Maybe Kitty was involved in their case.

Terry shuddered and let out a long breath.

Then she opened her purse. "I took Kurt's notes to review for tonight's rehearsal. I might as well stay out here on deck and look at them." She pulled out a wad of papers and started to read.

Suddenly a gust of wind kicked up and the notes flew out of her hands. Nancy grabbed for them before they sailed overboard. "That was close," Nancy said, holding them out.

Terry didn't reach for the papers even though her eyes were focused on them.

"Terry? What is it?" Bess asked.

When Terry didn't answer, Nancy glanced down at the top note—and gasped.

Flipping through the other papers, Nancy saw a single word had been scrawled in heavy, blood-red marking pen on each sheet.

The single word was *QUIT*.

Chapter

Seven

"Oh, no!" Bess exclaimed, gazing at the papers with horror.

Nancy's mind was already racing, trying to piece together who could be responsible. "You put the notes in your purse yesterday, at the theater?" she asked Terry, who nodded.

"Where was your purse?" Nancy asked.

"In my dressing room," Terry replied. "I left it there during rehearsal."

"Was the room locked?" Bess asked.

Terry shook her head. "I haven't been bothering. Pretty dumb, huh?"

Anyone could have done it, Nancy realized. The harassment was definitely picking up as the opening of the show grew closer. "We'll be more careful from now on," Nancy said, trying to reassure Terry.

"Don't worry," Bess said. "If anyone can find out who's behind this, it's Nancy."

Nancy smiled at Bess and Terry, but she didn't feel terribly confident.

The boat shuddered as it slowed down. "We're here!" Bess called. "And look, Frank, Joe, and Pat are waiting."

Pat hugged Terry and then pulled out a newspaper. "Look. We made page one."

Nancy peeked over Terry's shoulder to the newspaper Pat was holding. There was a photo of the couple smiling, one of Pat staring at the ugly stain on his jacket, and one of Pat and Alan glaring at each other, nose to nose.

"Any publicity is good, right?" Pat said with a laugh, but his voice sounded strained to Nancy. "How was last night?" he asked. Before Terry could answer, he said, "You can tell me over breakfast. I need to eat—my match is at one."

Terry gave the others a weak smile. "Have fun, guys. See you at the match."

"Is Terry upset about something?" Joe asked as the couple walked away.

Nancy filled them in on the blackout at the theater and the notes with the word *quit.* "It's like a nightmare she can't wake up from," she concluded.

"Pat didn't seem to have a clue," Bess said, slightly annoyed.

Joe shrugged. "Don't be too tough on the guy. He has his own troubles." Then he told her and Bess about Pat's gear being trashed.

"How's Pat doing?" she asked when they were done.

"He's jumpy," replied Frank. "We're doing the best we can to protect him, but Pat's got a lot of enemies." He sighed.

"Bess and I found out something that might help your case," Nancy said as they walked toward the tennis courts. She told them the story of Pat and Kitty's stormy breakup.

"I can't believe Pat didn't tell us about that. Now we have another name on the Pat Flynn Enemy List," Frank said, opening the gate to the court.

"He collects them like stamps," Joe replied, frowning. "Come on, you guys, I need to play some tennis!"

"The stands are totally full," Bess said a few hours later.

It was just before one o'clock, and several thousand spectators had filled McCallum Island's main tennis arena. Nancy, Bess, and Terry had excellent seats at the center of the court.

They were saving Frank and Joe's seats. The boys had gone off to the clubhouse to check on Pat.

"Just a few more minutes till the match starts. I feel so nervous." Terry glanced down at her clasped hands. "I'm sitting here wondering what awful thing will happen to me or Pat next. He's ready to snap from the hassling."

"Does he know what's been happening with you?" Nancy asked.

Terry shook her head. "I haven't given him the details. I didn't want to worry him. He has enough on his mind, playing in front of thousands of people. If he makes mistakes, he has to live with them."

"You have to do that in *Beauty,*" Bess pointed out.

"I'm not competing against someone, so the pressure's not the same," Terry said. "Pat worries that maybe *this* time Alan might be too good and beat him. I *know* I can do the show, no matter what Logan thinks."

Nancy admired Terry's confidence and said, "Does Logan's attitude bother you?"

Terry became grim. "I used to figure he was looking out for me. But I don't want to hear his negative thoughts anymore. If he doesn't let up—"

"You'd consider replacing him?" Nancy finished, aware of the resentment that had built up in Terry.

"Well . . . I would. Unless he cleans up his act." It sounded to Nancy as if Terry herself was surprised by her decision.

"There are Joe and Frank," Bess said, waving them up to their seats. A minute later they were settled comfortably between Nancy and Bess.

"Just in time," Frank said as Pat and Alan walked onto the grass. The crowd began cheering wildly. Nancy noticed that the two players didn't even glance at each other. They just moved to opposite ends of the court to warm up. In the hot sun, it didn't take them long.

The announcer introduced the players, and Alan smiled and waved. Pat was stone-faced, ignoring the mixture of applause and boos. To Nancy, it seemed as if the fans were evenly divided between the two.

"Pat looks grim," Nancy commented to Terry.

"It must be nerves," the actress replied, leaning forward, her arms on her knees.

"I'd sure be nervous," said Bess. "Look at all those TV cameras."

Half a dozen TV crews were taping the match. Although the exhibition didn't affect their rankings, whenever Pat and Alan played, the media paid attention. They were the best.

The crowd became almost silent as the game started. Pat served to the corner of the service box. Alan answered with a crosscourt backhand. With lightning reflexes, Pat darted left and smashed the ball down the line. Alan's passing shot looked to Nancy as if it was just inside the baseline for a winner.

"Love-fifteen," the umpire announced.

"Are you blind?" Pat screamed. "That ball was out by six inches! Come on!"

"Love-fifteen," the umpire repeated. "Play on, Mr. Flynn."

Muttering, Pat retreated to the serving line. Alan totally missed Pat's topspin serve. Now the score was fifteen all.

On the next point Pat followed his serve to the net. Alan tried a lob, but Pat put away an overhead smash. "Thirty-fifteen," Joe murmured.

Pat's next serve was called out by a line judge. Pat stared in disbelief at the judge.

"Second serve," the umpire said. This time, Alan slammed the ball back, and Pat fouled out. The crowd cheered loudly for Alan.

The next point was a marathon. Alan's reach was balanced by Pat's speed. Finally Pat won with a perfect crosscourt shot that left Alan stretched facedown on the court. There was applause as Pat prepared to serve at forty-thirty, game point.

"Come on, Pat!" Terry yelled, clapping her hands.

After another long volley, Pat hit a ball that

caught the tape on top of the net and dropped softly into Alan's court.

In the next game Alan served two straight aces. Then Pat moved back a few feet to receive and won a point. The score was thirty-fifteen. He let Alan's next serve go, turning expectantly to the line judge. The judge said nothing, and the umpire gave the point to Alan.

"Are you kidding?" Pat screamed. He pointed to a spot beyond the baseline. "Here's where it hit!" he shouted, marching to the spot. "Here's the mark!" He banged his racquet down on the court.

"Play on, Mr. Flynn," said the umpire as the catcalls from the crowd grew louder.

Nancy heard Terry whisper softly, "Stop it, Pat."

Pat raised his racquet and hit the baseline again, but then stopped and stood perfectly still.

"*Now* what?" Joe asked Frank.

"What's the matter?" murmured Terry, clutching Nancy's arm.

Nancy couldn't be sure, but something seemed to be very wrong. Pat swayed. Then slowly his arm dropped and his racquet fell to the court. His knees buckled, and he collapsed, his face an agonized mask.

Chapter
Eight

"P AT! WHAT'S HAPPENED to him?" Terry's frightened voice rang out as the crowd began to chant "Pat!"

"We've got to get down there!" Joe shouted, jumping up. Frank was right behind him. He, Nancy, Bess, and Terry pushed through to the aisle then ran down to the court.

A group that included Pat's coach and trainer, Butch, Kitty, and Gunnar was already with Pat when Terry and the others reached him.

"Honey, what's wrong? Pat? *Pat!*" Terry said, kneeling over her boyfriend.

Pat was gasping in pain. Sweat beaded his

forehead, his face was gray, and his teeth clenched. "My stomach," he said as a spasm racked his body.

Frank met Joe's eyes, and knew they were wondering the same thing. Was this more foul play?

Butch had gone to the PA system, and now they heard his voice blaring out over the loud-speakers.

"Ladies and gentlemen, please remain seated."

"Let me through," said a middle-aged woman as she pushed her way into the knot of people surrounding Pat. "I'm the tournament doctor," she said, and got down on one knee beside Pat.

Terry gave her a pleading look. "Will he be all right?" she begged.

"Pat, I'm Dr. Walsh, can you tell me what happened?" the doctor said, ignoring everyone but Pat.

"First I felt queasy," Pat said weakly. Frank could barely hear him. "I tried to play through it, but then these incredibly sharp stomach pains hit me."

"How long ago did you last eat?" the doctor asked.

"About two hours," Terry answered. "He had orange juice, pancakes, and scrambled eggs."

Everyone stood back as the doctor examined Pat. Before she was done, an ambulance drew to a stop beside the court, its siren blaring.

After the doctor had spoken to the paramedics and helped them settle Pat on the gurney, Frank approached her. "Dr. Walsh, do you have any idea what caused Pat to collapse?" he asked.

"A big meal and hard exercise on a hot day could account for it," she replied. "Of course, tests will show if it was that, or something else."

"Like what?" Joe asked, coming up beside Frank.

Dr. Walsh hesitated before saying, "Pat's symptoms are consistent with food poisoning."

The paramedics were rolling Pat's gurney toward the ambulance.

Frank nudged Joe to look at Alan and Gunnar, who were talking quietly on the sidelines. "They're pretty calm."

Joe nodded. "Yeah."

Frank watched and listened carefully as Alan and Gunnar made their way over to Butch. "What about our match? Can we reschedule?" Alan was asking.

Butch stared at Alan. "We can't discuss that *now*. We don't know when or even *if* Pat will be able to play again."

"He'll be fine," Gunnar said calmly.

"What makes you so sure?" Joe demanded, staring hard at the trainer.

"It is my profession. Already I see signs of recovery. His breathing gets less labored, color returns to his face."

Frank glanced at Pat as he was being lifted into the ambulance. He *did* look a little better. Still, Gunnar was taking this awfully lightly. Why?

"If you're right," Butch said, "and Pat is up to playing in a day or two, we'll arrange it then."

Terry tried to get into the ambulance, but a paramedic stopped her. "It's too crowded. Meet us at the infirmary, by the main lodge."

"We'll go with you," said Bess.

As they started to walk away they heard Kitty say to Butch, "How are our teenage detectives doing? Have they solved the case? No? Somehow, I'm not surprised. Why don't you get rid of them and hire professionals?"

"That's it," said Joe, turning to confront Kitty.

Frank caught Joe's arm. "Easy, little brother. You'll get us thrown off the case if you lose your temper."

"Kitty really is on your case," Nancy said as they walked to the infirmary.

"You noticed, huh?" Joe replied.

"Amazing, isn't it? I mean, how could any woman dump on a hunk like Joe?" Frank teased. He was still thinking about what Dr. Walsh had said about food poisoning. "Where did you guys eat this morning?" he asked Terry.

"The Seaview Grill," she told him.

That made sense, Frank thought. The exhibition had a contract with the restaurant owner, and the players ate all their meals there.

"Was there anything unusual about what Pat ate this morning?" Joe asked.

"No, except how much food he put away. He said he had to fuel up, and that if the match took a long time, he didn't want to fade early."

Frank caught Joe's eye. "Let's check the Seaview Grill. If anyone else had a bad reaction to the food today, then this probably wasn't an attack on Pat. We can scope out the kitchen."

"We'll go to the infirmary," said Nancy.

"Come on," Terry said. "I'm really worried about Pat."

"Doesn't look like the kind of place that would serve spoiled food," Joe said as he and Frank surveyed the Seaview Grill. It was a classy, sparkling clean restaurant.

When they asked for the chef, the brothers were taken into an equally spotless kitchen. A heavyset middle-aged man in a snowy apron and tall, stiff cap was introduced as the chef. His face was dominated by thick, bristling eyebrows, which knit together when Joe explained why they had come.

"You think *I* poisoned this tennis player?" the chef roared. Around the room, people busy preparing food turned at the outburst.

"We're not accusing you—" Frank began.

"We use the best ingredients! I inspect them myself! Every piece of meat, every egg, every clove of garlic! No one gets sick from my food—ever!"

Joe jumped in, trying to soothe the chef. "We didn't mean—"

"This kitchen is spotless! You could eat off this floor!"

"It's just that—" Joe tried again.

"That's enough!" The chef waved his knife. "I cannot, *will not* serve tennis people anymore. They can use the snack bar."

Joe exchanged a look of dismay with his brother. He turned as the kitchen door pushed open and frowned when he saw who it was.

"Frank! Joe! They told me you came in here," Kitty said, moving toward them. "Just what are you doing?"

"Our job," Frank replied evenly.

"They insulted me!" the chef shouted. "Never will I cook for tennis players—"

Kitty glared at the Hardys and linked her arm through the chef's. "Michel, don't deprive us of your food. We *love* it. Everyone raves about it. I would kill for your recipe for bouillabaisse."

A grin lit up Michel's face. Joe had to admire Kitty as she worked on the guy. "Ah, you appreciate fine things," the chef purred.

"We admire true artistry." Kitty's smile would have melted ice. "Michel, I'll have a word with these two. There won't be further problems. Come on," she said, eyeing the Hardys coldly.

As soon as they were out of the kitchen, Kitty said, "What's *wrong* with you? Why did you pester Michel? Couldn't you see he was temperamental?"

"Now we can," Joe said.

"A Consolidated executive called me after seeing a news item about Pat and Alan arguing," Kitty said angrily. "He was unhappy. We don't *want* our sponsor unhappy. Consolidated is very image conscious, and they have a clause in their contract that will allow them to pull out as sponsors if we get any bad publicity. Michel can stir things up, and we can't afford that. Am I clear?"

"Very," Frank said.

"Now, go back in and apologize to him."

Joe opened his mouth to object, but closed it when he checked with Frank. "Okay," Frank said. "Maybe talking to him wasn't such a hot idea."

Going back inside the kitchen, Frank, Joe, and Kitty approached the chef. Frank cleared his throat. "Sorry, Michel. We didn't mean to upset you."

The chef was stirring a vat of soup without glancing at the Hardys. "Special diets, intruders in my kitchen, and now *you*—" he grumbled.

Frank caught Joe's eye. "You mean people just wander in and out? That must be frustrating."

Michel rolled his eyes. "You have no idea. One even had the gall to add things to the food."

"That's too much." Joe urged the chef on. "Was he here today?"

"Yes, like always."

"We'll tell Butch to speak with him," Frank said. "What's his name?"

"I don't know, but he has long brown hair. Also, a droopy mustache."

Joe tried not to let his excitement show. Michel had just described Gunnar Hedstrom.

Chapter
Nine

WHAT HAD GUNNAR put in the food? Had he poisoned Pat? Frank wanted to ask more questions, but before he could, Kitty was hustling them out. "Michel has work to do."

"Okay," Frank agreed. He didn't want to get Kitty or Michel any angrier. "We're out of here, Joe. Come on, let's check on Pat."

A few minutes later they joined Nancy, Bess, Terry, and a couple of reporters in the waiting room.

"How's he doing?" Frank asked Nancy.

"We're waiting to hear," she replied. "Did you learn anything at the restaurant?"

"We talked to the chef," Frank said.

"It turns out that a man has been hanging around the kitchen, adding things to the food," Frank went on. "From the chef's description, it sounds as if it was Gunnar."

"Gunnar . . ." Nancy repeated. "Doctoring food?"

Frank nodded. "We can't be sure, but—"

He broke off as Dr. Walsh came in. Terry jumped up and hurried over to her. "How is Pat? Is he all right?"

The doctor smiled. "He'll be fine. He's no longer in severe pain, though he *is* quite weak."

"What caused it?" Joe asked.

"Mild food poisoning," Dr. Walsh answered. "We won't know exactly what the problem was until we get a lab analysis of what he ate."

"Can we see him?" asked Terry.

"Okay," the doctor finally relented. "But not for long, and not all together."

"Tell you what," Joe said to Frank. "I'll look for Gunnar and you talk to Pat."

Bess decided to go with Joe. Dr. Walsh led the others down a long hallway. "Here we are," she said, opening a door at the end of the corridor and ushering them inside. "I'll leave you alone now."

Pat smiled weakly at them from the bed. Terry instantly claimed the chair beside the bed and took Pat's hand.

Frank stood at the foot of the bed. "If you feel up to it, we should talk a little," he said gently.

"Sure." Although Pat sounded tired, his eyes were alert.

Frank quickly told him about Gunnar being in the kitchen and perhaps tampering with the food. Pat's eyes narrowed as he listened, and his jaw clenched.

"Gunnar," he exclaimed angrily. "What did I tell you? He's up to something."

"Whoa, easy," Frank urged. "You're supposed to be resting, remember? Tell us about you and Gunnar."

"He coached me for a year and a half," Pat said. "Gunnar knows tennis, I'll give him that. But he always nagged me. Told me I wasn't serious enough, I went out too much, I lost my temper too much. We had huge fights. And he's a nut about food."

"How do you mean?" Nancy asked.

Pat nodded. "Nutrition. His training diet drove me crazy. No red meat, dairy products, or desserts. Plain fish, steamed veggies—boring beyond belief. But the worst was the food supplements he used."

Frank asked, "He'd add them to meals?"

"Right. They made boring food even worse. He'd whip up health drinks in a blender, too. With wheat germ, liver extract, yeast, lecithin, uh, aloe vera juice, and who knows what all. He's like a walking pharmacy, with his trunkful of bottles and cans and jars. I had to drink a couple of his concoctions every day. Yuck!

"One day after I lost a tough match, he started in on me. He said I deserved to lose, I hadn't worked out enough, blah, blah, blah. Well, I lost it. I told him I was sick of lectures and health drinks, too. He said that while he was my coach I'd do what I was told. So I said, 'Then you're *not* my coach. You're fired.' Maybe I shouldn't have done it, but I was sore."

"Uh-huh." Frank looked at Nancy. "So maybe Gunnar was just putting supplements in Alan's food in the kitchen—"

"Or he could have been doctoring Pat's food," Nancy finished.

Frank grinned at her. "You got it." Then he noticed that Pat and Terry were no longer paying attention, but staring only at each other. They probably wanted some time alone. "Let's get some fresh air," Frank said to Nancy. "Terry, we'll wait outside."

Frank and Nancy went outside and sat on a wooden bench in front of the infirmary.

"So, do you think Gunnar did it?" Nancy asked.

Frank shrugged. "Maybe. Or maybe Gunnar and Alan are involved together."

"Poor Terry," Nancy said. "She finally gets to see Pat after two months, and has to settle for a few minutes alone in an infirmary room."

"If we're lucky, we'll find Gunnar in here," Joe told Bess as they came to a sleek structure of steel and glass. A sign identified it as the VIP Clubhouse. Distant applause and crowd noise indicated that another tennis match was in progress. "It's reserved for tour personnel."

"Pretty impressive," Bess said as Joe pushed open the glass doors, and they stepped inside. The sleek lobby was empty, except for some couches and a table strewn with magazines. Arrows pointed to the exercise room, sauna, training room, and men's and women's locker rooms.

"You see if he's in the locker room, and I'll wait here." Bess sat on a couch.

"Okay," Joe answered. "It won't take long."

After pushing through the locker room door, Joe glanced quickly at the rows of lockers, benches, and showers. The place was empty. Everyone's at the match, he thought, glancing at a steel whirlpool through a tiled archway. He was about to leave when something caught his eye. "Hey, what's this?" Joe murmured.

On the floor beside the exit was a large canvas athletic bag, its top open. He must have overlooked it when he stepped inside. The name tag attached to the handle read "GUNNAR HEDSTROM." Might as well take a quick look through, Joe decided.

It was full of labeled containers. Squatting, he searched the contents, reading labels: lecithin, liver extract, papaya enzyme. Looks like a bunch of weird vitamins, Joe thought. But why were they sitting here?

Joe paused as his eye fell on a bottle marked only with a large black X. It contained a white powder. Joe studied the bottle closely. The chef at the Seaview Grill had said that Gunnar had been in the kitchen—adding supplements to food! All of the bottles here were carefully labeled—except this one. Could Gunnar have used this powder to poison Pat? Joe decided to take a sample and have its contents analyzed.

Pulling a plastic bag from his pocket, he unscrewed the bottle top and poured some of the powder into the bag. Then he screwed the cap back on and put it back where he had found it. He stuffed the plastic bag in his pocket, glad to have been lucky.

Just as he started to rise, two large and powerful hands clamped down hard on his shoulders. "What?" Caught off guard, Joe tried to wrench free, but he was lifted bodily off the floor and flung against the nearby lockers. He turned around and found himself staring into Alan Lassiter's furious face. Uh-oh, Joe thought. Had Alan seen him take the sample?

"What are you doing?" Alan snapped, fists clenched at his sides. "Where did you get Gunnar's stuff, and why were you messing around with it?"

"I found the bag right here," Joe replied. "I just looked to see whose it was."

"Yeah, right," Alan sneered. "You must think I'm pretty dumb to hand me that. I've had my eye on you and your brother since you got here. Don't think you'll get away with it!"

"Get away with what?" Joe moved away from the lockers to give himself room in case Alan decided to fight.

"Come off it," Alan said. "Pat wants to put us on the spot, and you're helping him out. Now, what were you doing with Gunnar's stuff?"

Joe held up his hands, realizing that Alan hadn't seen him take the sample. "You're wrong. Frank and I are only trying to protect Pat from—"

"Save your breath! Look, if you make trouble for us, you'll get trouble back—with interest."

Something about Alan's words made no sense to Joe. *"Pat's* the one getting harassed, not you."

"And you think you're going to pin it on Gunnar and me, huh? Think again, dude!"

When Alan launched a roundhouse right toward Joe's jaw, Joe was ready. He pulled back, and the punch whistled past his mouth. He threw a short left that landed under Alan's ribs and backed him up a step. Alan dropped into a fighter's stance, fists cocked, and feinted toward Joe.

Just then there was a knock on the locker room door. Bess poked her head in. "Joe?" she called. "Are you all right? What's going on?"

Alan's head snapped around toward the door. As soon as he saw Bess, he unclenched his hands. "Saved by your girl," he said. "Get out of here. Next time, you won't be so lucky."

"You're the lucky one, Lassiter," Joe shot back. "I'll be right there," he told Bess, and she ducked back outside. Joe headed for the exit, but paused before leaving.

"The firecracker, the water pistol, and the food poisoning all happened to Pat. If you're the target, why is Pat the one getting hit?"

Alan shrugged. "Knowing Pat, he could've arranged it himself," he said, "to get his name and picture plastered all over the place." He turned his back on Joe, who headed outside.

"Are you okay?" Bess asked. "I saw Alan go in there and heard shouting. Did I do right, calling you?"

Joe grinned. "Definitely. I owe you one. How about I pay you back by buying you dinner tomorrow night?" Joe asked.

"Great," Bess replied. "What happened in there anyway?"

"Let's walk and talk," Joe suggested. "We should probably get back to the infirmary." As they made their way across the resort, he told Bess about the unidentified powder in Gunnar's bag.

When Bess and Joe arrived at the infirmary, they found Butch and Terry perched beside Pat's bed. Nancy and Frank weren't there.

"I feel better, and the doc says I can leave in a few hours," Pat said when Joe asked how he was. "I can play tomorrow, I think."

"Whoa," Butch said. "Don't rush things. I want you to see a specialist in Charleston and get a thorough examination. If you get a clean bill of health and you feel up to it, we'll arrange the match for tomorrow or the next day."

Terry gave her boyfriend's hand a squeeze. "I hate to leave now, but I have to get to rehearsal by four-thirty," she said.

"I'd better go, too," Butch said, checking his watch. "Kitty is waiting to brief the press."

Frank and Nancy entered just after Butch left. "We were getting something to drink," Frank explained. "Did you find Gunnar?"

"No, but I found this." Joe pulled out the bag of powder and explained how he had gotten it. "If this stuff turns out to be poison, we may be onto the attacker."

While Terry and Pat said goodbye, Nancy, Bess, Frank, and Joe waited outside.

"There's something weird I didn't mention in there," Joe said. "Alan thinks Pat organized the harassment campaign himself, to get publicity."

"*And* cast suspicion on Alan and Gunnar at the same time," Frank said. "Very neat."

"That sounds crazy," Bess put in.

"Maybe," Joe replied, "but it's possible."

Nancy sighed. "In other words, you have a new suspect—the guy you're trying to protect!"

Just then, Terry emerged from Pat's room. "Okay, he's all yours," she said to Frank and Joe.

The actress was quiet as the girls caught the boat back to the mainland. An hour later they were back at the Majestic Theater.

"Right on time!" Kurt said, brushing a hand through his sandy hair. "The wiring's fixed, and we have a lot to do. How did Pat do? Did he win?"

Frowning, Terry told him about Pat. "But he ought to be able to play tomorrow or the next day," she finished.

Kurt seemed concerned. "Are you all right? Pat's collapse must have upset you."

"It did, but he's fine now, and so am I."

Kurt grinned, but Nancy saw that he continued to study Terry intently. "You're sure?"

Terry answered him simply. "Positive."

"Okay, then." The director put his arm around her shoulders and squeezed.

Just then Logan appeared from the corridor to the dressing rooms. "Oh, you're here," he said to Terry. "I was coming to look for you."

"Look for me? Why?" Terry said coolly. "I'm always on time for work."

"Sure," he replied quickly, focusing down at the floor. "Uh, how was the tennis?"

"Not great," she said. Turning to Kurt, she changed the subject. "What's on the schedule?"

Logan flushed. To Nancy, it seemed that his days as Terry's manager were numbered.

"I've got a few things I need to go over with you before we start," Kurt told Terry.

Terry nodded, then said to Logan, "We'll talk later." She took Kurt's arm, and they headed in the direction of the stage.

Logan stood and gnawed on his lower lip. Nancy felt uncomfortable witnessing the argument. Clearing her throat, she said, "If you have a few minutes, Logan, I'd like to ask you a few things."

At first she thought he hadn't heard her, then Logan said, "Sure, why not."

As Nancy, Logan, and Bess started for Terry's dressing room, Nancy said, "There are a few questions that— Logan? What is it?"

He had stopped abruptly and was staring at

Terry's dressing room door, which was slightly ajar. "I left that door locked," he said, frowning.

From inside the room, Nancy could hear a scraping noise, like furniture being moved. She gestured to Logan and Bess to be quiet.

Nancy peered through the narrow opening of the door, but saw no one.

Her heart pounded as she gently pushed the door. It swung silently open.

Inside, a man was standing with his back to the door. He was holding a small tube of red lipstick.

Over his shoulder, Nancy saw a jagged red scrawl across the face of the mirror that read "R.I.P., TERRY!"

Behind her, she heard Bess gasp. Nancy caught her breath as the man whirled around to face them. It was Warren Brophy!

Chapter

Ten

WARREN BROPHY'S EYES were wide and his mouth was a round *O* as Nancy moved toward him.

Just then Logan lurched past her and grabbed the playwright. "I'll break your neck!" Logan yelled.

"Get him off me!" Brophy screamed.

Nancy grabbed Logan's arm and bent it up sharply behind his back.

"Cut that out! It hurts!" Logan cried out.

Nancy released his arm. "Back off, Logan. Now."

Logan remained still for an instant, his eyes

boring into Brophy's. Then, to Nancy's relief, he stepped back.

"Okay, Mr. Brophy, tell us what you were doing here," Nancy said, staring hard at the playwright. "And how did you get in? The door was locked."

Brophy stiffened, acting outraged. "It was *not* locked. I don't break into locked rooms. I'm here for an interview—"

"That's a lie!" Logan shouted.

Exasperated, Nancy threw up her hands. "This will be simpler if you keep out of it, Logan."

The manager gave Nancy a sullen nod and leaned against the wall, hands shoved in his pants pockets.

"Go on," Nancy told the writer.

"I'm doing an article on *Beauty and the Beat* for *Lively Arts Monthly.* I wrote asking for an interview, and Terry sent word to meet her here," Brophy explained. "I got here five minutes ago, found this bizarre message and the lipstick with which it had obviously been written. I had just picked up the lipstick when you burst in."

"You talked to Terry today?" Bess asked.

Warren Brophy shook his head. "No, she left a message at my hotel this morning."

"I don't think so," Nancy put in. "She never mentioned a word about an interview."

"What?" Brophy's eyes widened. "But—"

Just then the door opened and Terry, Kurt, and

Stuart entered. Seeing the scrawl on the mirror, Terry gasped. "Not again. Please, not again."

"Nancy, what's going on?" Stuart asked, staring at Brophy. "Who let *him* in?"

"We found him standing in front of the mirror, with that message already on it," Nancy explained. "He says he had an appointment to interview Terry and that the mirror was that way when he got here."

Terry shook her head, still staring at the mirror. "I didn't make any appointment with him."

Stuart jabbed a finger at Brophy. "This man is trying to wreck my show."

"He's right," exclaimed Logan.

"That's a lie," Brophy retorted hotly. "You hate my guts because I've exposed you as an overrated fraud who pollutes the theater, and—"

"You miserable phony!" Stuart started to advance on Brophy, but Kurt pulled him back.

"Stop it!" Nancy yelled. The room suddenly grew silent. Nancy turned to Terry and asked, "Do you want to talk to Brophy?"

"No," she said, taking a towel from the table and rubbing at the crimson threat on the mirror. "I don't want anything to do with him."

"You heard her. Get out of here," Stuart growled.

Brophy gave Stuart a venomous look and said, "Gladly. You'll *love* my new article, Firman. It

will expose you for the sleazy hack you are."
With that, he stalked out, slamming the dressing
room door.

"Wow! Talk about angry!" Bess exclaimed.

Nancy watched Terry, who was still rubbing
the mirror with the towel, even though the words
were no longer legible.

"Terry, you could avoid all this by getting out
of the show," Logan pointed out.

"Enough!" Terry flared. "Logan, lately all you
do is snipe at the show and make remarks about
my getting out of it. Don't you want me to be
happy?"

Logan reached for Terry's hand, which she
pulled away. "Everything I do is for you," he
exclaimed. "All I care about is what's good for
you. You know that, don't you?"

Terry just stared silently at him until finally he
sputtered to a stop. Nancy had been struck by the
intensity of his outburst.

"Let's hurry, Frank," Joe said the next afternoon as they hustled down the fluorescent-lit
hallway of the hospital in Charleston. "Pat
wasn't happy about spending last night here for
observation. He'll kill us if we're a second late to
get him out of here."

Although Pat had sustained a mild case of food
poisoning, there would be no lasting effects.

Butch had rescheduled the exhibition match with Alan for the next day.

Frank let out a sigh of frustration as they moved along. "Too bad the lab won't have the results from that powder sample for a few more hours."

He stopped in front of a door marked 312. "Here we are." Taking a deep breath, he turned the knob and went in. He and Joe found Pat dressed and waiting for them. He was pacing back and forth, full of nervous energy.

"All right!" Pat said. "I'm officially healthy, and I'm going to go watch Terry's rehearsal. Then tomorrow I'm going to nail Lassiter. He won't know what hit him. He and Gunnar are going to pay for what they did to me. They'll need a lot more than yeast and liver extract to beat me!"

Pat was convinced Gunnar and Alan were behind the attacks, but Frank wasn't. In the cab to the theater Frank decided to ask Pat about Kitty Wills. They hadn't had a chance to talk about her yet.

"Tell us about you and Kitty," Frank said. "I'm not sure Alan and Gunnar are behind the attacks."

Pat glared at Frank. "I won't talk about Kitty," he said firmly.

"You've got to trust us, or we can't do our job," Joe argued.

Pat was quiet for a moment. Then he nodded

and said, "Okay. But you have to promise not to breathe a word of this, especially not to Terry."

"Terry?" Frank was surprised. "But she already knows that you went with Kitty before her. What's the big deal?"

Pat looked uneasily from Frank to Joe before answering. "What Terry doesn't know is that I started dating her as a public relations move."

"What?" Frank thought he had heard wrong.

"Terry can never find out," Pat insisted. "There's something else, too."

"What's that?" Joe asked.

"You're not going to like this, but"—Pat took a deep breath—"going out with Terry was Kitty's idea."

"You dated Terry for *publicity?*" Joe stared at Pat in disbelief.

Pat shrugged. "Kitty said I needed broader appeal and that Terry would get it for me."

"Uh-huh." Joe had to stop himself from decking Pat. What a sleaze.

"You'd better tell us the whole story," Frank urged.

"It started about a year and a half ago when I had a brawl with another player. I drew a six-month suspension. I couldn't play in any pro event."

Frank let out a whistle. "Sounds rough."

Pat shrugged. "I was a lot luckier than the other guy. Neal Ross had been in a lot of trouble before, so he got banned for life. He died two months later in a car crash. Some people say he did it on purpose."

"I remember Neal Ross," Joe said. "A lot of people thought he could have been the best in the world, right?"

"Right," Pat said.

"Where does Terry come in?" Frank asked.

"Kitty was my publicist then, as well as my girlfriend," Pat continued. "Because of the fight, two of my commercial contracts were dropped, and I lost a lot of money. When I was reinstated Kitty said I had to rebuild my image. Her idea was for me to date a girl who was known by the whole youth market. Kitty figured Terry'd be perfect because she had a huge PTV following. So I introduced myself, we talked, and I asked her out."

"I guess Kitty's plan worked," Frank said, trying not to show how turned off he was by Pat's story.

Pat nodded. "Absolutely! I got ads, new endorsements, the whole deal. What Kitty didn't expect was that I'd *like* Terry, but I did."

"So then you broke up with Kitty," Joe said. "I'll bet she was mad."

Pat grimaced. "It was ugly, but I knew she wouldn't tell Terry because it would make her look bad, too. At least she hasn't given me any grief on the tour. I guess she decided it isn't worth it—getting back at me."

"You can't be sure of that," Frank replied.

"I should never have agreed to this tour. It's been a drag from day one, between having to see Kitty and all the sabotage. I might just take off," Pat said.

"But you have a contract," Frank pointed out.

Pat waved dismissively. "No sweat. I could say I threw my back out. No specialist in the world could prove otherwise. That's the beauty of back injuries. One thing's for sure: Butch is going to have to sweeten my deal if he wants me to stay for the rest of the tournament."

Joe exchanged a glance with Frank. Pat was making himself look worse each time he opened his mouth. "Where would he get the extra money?" Frank asked. "From Consolidated Motors?"

"Why not?" Pat asked, shrugging. "They can afford it. Butch says he's working on it."

Joe was relieved when they reached the theater a minute later. He couldn't take any more of Pat and his selfish, sleazy attitude.

At the theater the boys were directed to the greenroom. The lounge turned out to be a cluttered but comfortable room full of unmatched pieces of old furniture in every color but green.

The girls were sitting with some of the cast at a

table covered with take-out food containers. When Bess saw Joe, her face lit up in a big welcoming smile. "Hi! We're still on for tonight, right?" Joe smiled. "I hope you're hungry, because I heard about a great restaurant called Fatback. It has fantastic down-home food, right, Cal?"

A thin young man in jeans and a T-shirt nodded and said, "For sure! The chicken and smothered steak are out of sight. It's Leese's favorite place."

"Cal's dating a local girl named Leese," Nancy explained. "Joe, Frank, Pat, meet Cal Lipton." Joe nodded as he was introduced to Kurt Zimmer, the director, and some of the stage crew. "The cast is on their dinner break," Nancy explained.

"Why is this called the greenroom?" Frank asked, sitting down in an empty chair. "Nothing in here is green."

Terry made room on her couch for Pat. "It's what they always call actors' lounges."

"Ready to go?" Joe asked Bess. "My stomach sure is."

"Sure."

"Have fun," Nancy said. "And bring me back some pecan pie!"

Nancy relaxed in her seat in the eighth row at the Majestic Theater to watch the final dress rehearsal for *Beauty and the Beat.* Bess and Joe were still out to dinner so Nancy and Frank were on their own for now. Frank chose to sit farther back, so he could take in the whole picture, he said. The show was going great, Nancy thought. It had wonderful songs and a clever story based on *Beauty and the Beast.*

"This is fun, huh?" a voice whispered in Nancy's ear, startling her. It was Pat. Nancy had been so engrossed in the show that she hadn't even noticed he had sat down next to her.

Nancy nodded, watching the stage. A minute later Pat spoke again. "I could give you a tennis lesson if you'd like," he said softly.

"Thanks," Nancy whispered, her eyes on Terry onstage. If I ignore him, she thought, he'll get the message that I want to watch the show.

She was wrong. Pat kept whispering to her, his voice too low to be heard by anyone else. "I could give you great tips. How about it?"

Nancy stared at him coldly. "No. Now, please cut it out and let me enjoy the show."

Nancy wondered if he always hit on girls like this. If he made one more comment, Nancy decided she'd have to change her seat.

At that moment someone else sat down on her other side. "Nan, I have to talk to you," came Leese's voice. Even in the darkness, Nancy could tell the other girl was upset. "Now? Please?"

"Okay," Nancy whispered. "Come on."

Moving as quietly as they could, the girls went outside to talk. Leese raised her red-rimmed eyes to Nancy.

"I don't know what to do," Leese blurted out. "I have to warn Terry."

"Warn her?" Nancy repeated. "About what?"

"I think my grandfather is mixed up in some horrible plan to ruin this show!" Leese answered.

"Relax and tell me about it," urged Nancy.

Leese leaned against a car and said, "Earlier today on my way out of the house I went past the den. The doors were closed, but I heard Grandpa talking with someone. I heard him say, 'Is Terry Alford really on the verge of quitting the show?' Then he said, 'Well, maybe we can give her a little push.'"

It sounded as if Beau Tolliver was mixed up in a shady scheme, Nancy thought. But with whom? He didn't seem like the type who would resort to anonymous threats and physical assaults. Maybe that was the accomplice's doing. "Did you see or hear the other person?" Nancy asked.

"No. I wanted to listen more, but I heard someone coming so I took off."

"So your grandfather doesn't know you overheard him?" asked Nancy.

"Nope," Leese answered. "I got out of there right away. Nobody saw me, I'm pretty sure. What'll I do?" she asked, blinking back a tear.

"He's my grandfather, Nancy. Maybe he's totally innocent. But if not, I can't stand by and let Terry be hurt."

Nancy took Leese's hand in both of hers. "Try not to let it worry you. We'll get to the bottom of this."

Just then Nancy saw a car pull into the lot. It came to a stop, and Bess and Joe got out.

"Is rehearsal over?" Bess asked, sounding disappointed.

"Not yet," Nancy said.

"Joe, meet Leese Tolliver. She's the one who told me about Fatback," Bess added.

"No kidding?" Joe said. "Thanks a lot! That was the best dinner I've had since we got to South Carolina."

Leese barely acknowledged Joe. "What's wrong?" Bess asked. When Nancy told Bess and Joe what Leese had heard her grandfather say, Bess gave Leese a look of sympathy. "You must feel terrible!"

"So what do we do now?" asked Leese, shivering.

"I need to know more about what your grandfather meant, for starters," Nancy told her. "But you look like you're getting cold. Let's go inside, someplace where we can talk."

"How about the greenroom?" Leese suggested.

Nancy shook her head. "Too public. Terry's

dressing room would be perfect, but we'd be in the way there."

"Actually, she doesn't go there after the middle of the second act," Leese said. "She's onstage most of the time and makes her changes in the wings."

"Okay then," Nancy agreed. "Let's go."

"I should find Frank," Joe said.

"He's watching the rehearsal," Nancy said, then told him how to get to the front of the house. With a quick wave, he disappeared down the hallway.

"Dinner was fantastic, but I wish I'd seen the whole show," Bess said. "How is it?"

Nancy stopped and sighed. "It's really good," she replied. "I wish I could have concentrated on it, but Pat Flynn kept talking to me. He was actually hitting on me."

Bess stared. *"Pat?* You're kidding! Right under his girlfriend's nose? Poor Terry. What did you do?"

"I told him to chill out. I was about to move when Leese came up."

Looking ahead down the hallway, Nancy saw Logan heading their way. "Do you think it's okay if we use Terry's dressing room?" she asked him.

Logan seemed doubtful. "I don't know. The thing is, we're keeping the room locked for security reasons. Isn't there another place you can go?"

"Not one that's private," Bess told him.

"Well, okay." Logan went to the doorman for Terry's key. "Here."

"Thanks," Nancy told him. "See you."

"I'm telling you," Bess said as the three girls walked down the hall to the dressing room. "Warren Brophy is mixed up in this, somehow. Maybe he talked Beau into— Oh!"

As Bess rounded a corner, she almost bumped into Holly Bartell. Terry's understudy backed away, startled.

"Oops, sorry about that," she whispered, playing nervously with a strand of dark hair. She darted a quick glance back the way she had come. "Uh, what are you doing back here?"

"Going to Terry's dressing room," replied Nancy.

"But"—Holly shook her head—"you can't! I mean, they keep it locked."

"We have the key," Nancy said, wondering why Holly was so nervous. "And we have permission to use the room."

"Well, okay." She shrugged. "We're being real careful backstage lately. Well, I've got to hurry. A big number's coming up, and I want to watch. 'Bye!" She took off at a near-run.

Nancy stared after her, puzzled. "She was

watching the run-through from the house, earlier," she told Bess and Leese. "I wonder what brought her backstage in the middle of the show? Here we are."

Nancy stopped outside the door to Terry's dressing room and held up the key Logan had gotten from the doorman. "We'll get settled in here, then go over everything you heard your grandfather say one more time."

Nancy turned the key and swung the door open. The dressing room was dark as she groped for a light switch. "Don't worry, Leese, we'll sort this out," she said, trying to reassure the girl.

"Great," Leese said, as Nancy flipped the switch. The overhead lights went on, and Nancy stood back to allow the other girls to enter.

Leese and Bess stepped past her into the room.

Nancy started to say something, but her words were cut off by a loud explosion. The whole room erupted in a searing flash of light and dense white smoke!

Chapter

Eleven

NANCY STAGGERED BACK, coughing and feeling completely disoriented. All she could see were stars. It was a bomb, she thought, blinking furiously. As her vision began to clear, she tried to peer through the smoke.

"Bess! Leese! Can you hear me?" she shouted, her heart pounding. They had been all the way in the room and must have gotten the full impact from the blast. Were they lying hurt and helpless in that thick white cloud?

"Bess!" she called again more urgently. *"Leese!"*

Suddenly Bess staggered out into the hall and

bumped into Nancy, clutching her arms. "Nan? What happened?" she asked.

Nancy heard coughing from inside the dressing room. She stared into the thinning smoke and saw Leese standing stock-still as if paralyzed.

Nancy raced inside to help the girl out of the room. Leese took Nancy's hand and moved slowly. She blinked and gave a short cry. "I can't see!"

"I couldn't either, at first. It's only temporary," Nancy assured her. "It must have been some kind of smoke bomb." She ducked back into the dressing room, got a chair, and placed it in the corridor for Leese to sit on.

Both Leese and Bess were badly shaken, but both girls could see now and were basically uninjured. Nancy reentered the room. Everything was intact. Then her eye caught a smoldering pile of ash beside the old couch. A patch of upholstery near the pile had been singed.

Nancy looked up as two girls from the chorus appeared in the doorway. "What happened?" asked one. "We smelled something burning." She stopped short and gaped at the singed couch. "A fire!"

"No, nothing like that," Nancy said quickly. "But I think you'd better find Tim to tell him there's a problem in here."

"You mean—stop the run-through?" the other dancer asked doubtfully.

"It's an emergency," Nancy insisted. "I'll take full responsibility. Please hurry."

The dancers raced toward the stage. Less than a minute later, they returned with Tim Delevan, his headset hanging around his neck.

"What's going on?" he asked. "We're not supposed to stop this run-through for any reason . . ."

His voice trailed off and he sniffed the air. "Someone's been setting off flash powder."

"Is that what it is?" Bess asked, crinkling up her nose.

"No mistaking that smell," he answered.

"What is it, and how does it work?" Nancy wanted to know.

"It's aluminum hydroxide," Tim explained. "It's used for special effects. You set it off with a spark, and it gives you light and smoke but no fire. It's safe to work with onstage."

Nancy frowned. "It was a booby trap," she said. "It was set to go off when the lights were turned on. My guess is that it was intended to frighten, not to cause injury," she said, thinking aloud. "It was meant to scare Terry."

"But the room was locked," Bess pointed out. "How did the person get in?"

"Good question," Nancy agreed. "And who did it?" She tightened her jaw into a determined line.

* * *

Frank looked up as Joe sat down next to him. "How's the show?" Joe asked.

"Good, I guess," Frank whispered. "I was distracted for a little while watching another show a few rows ahead, and I didn't like it at all." Scowling, he motioned to where Pat was sitting by himself.

"He sat down next to Nancy and started hitting on her," Frank said. "It was unbelievable!"

"Terry's nice. She deserves better than Pat," Joe said.

"You got *that* right," Frank muttered. "The guy is the pits, and here we are, trying to protect him. I'd like to deck him myself!"

Joe was amazed. Frank didn't often show such strong emotions. "Don't let him get to you. When this case is over, you can tell Pat what you think of him."

Frank nodded grimly. "He'd better be wearing a mouthpiece when we have *that* little talk. Nancy left a while ago with some girl, by the way."

"Right, I saw them," Joe said. He told Frank about Leese and her suspicions of her grandfather.

"Maybe that's the breakthrough Nancy needs," Frank said.

"Can I have your attention, please?" Kurt's voice blared over the bullhorn. Frank glanced toward the stage. There was some confusion as Terry and the other performers stopped and stared into the house.

"I'm sorry to interrupt the run-through like this," the director continued. "Everything was going extremely well. A technical problem has come up backstage that I have to see to. Please, everyone, stay where you are. We'll pick up exactly where we left off in a few minutes. Thank you."

Kurt got up from the front of the audience and strode onto the stage. He conferred with Terry, and they disappeared into the wings.

Frank nudged Joe as Pat stood up and started down the aisle toward the stage, too.

"Pat's not too good at following orders," Joe said. "I wonder what's going on?"

"Let's follow him, Joe," Frank said. "It looks like we're going to find out."

"What happened here?" Kurt asked outside Terry's dressing room. Nancy could tell he wasn't pleased that his rehearsal had been interrupted. When he saw Terry's dressing room, however, his expression softened.

Terry stepped in after Kurt. As Nancy and Bess explained what had happened, Terry started trembling.

"Why is this happening?" Terry murmured, grabbing Kurt's arm.

The director put his arm protectively around Terry. "Any idea who did this?" Kurt asked Nancy.

Nancy had some ideas, but didn't want to speak openly with people around. "Nothing definite," she hedged.

A few moments later the Hardys and Pat appeared. "What's going on?" Joe asked, poking his head into the dressing room.

Nancy gave them a quick summary. "Flash powder, huh?" Frank said.

"We have a supply in a storeroom," Tim explained.

"Better see if any's been taken," Kurt suggested to Tim, who took off.

Terry was so preoccupied she hadn't even noticed Pat. Suddenly her eyes fell on her boyfriend and she ran into his arms.

"You okay, babe?" he asked. At least he acted concerned, Nancy thought. Not that it excused the way he'd flirted with her earlier.

"I'm not hurt, just shaken. I feel cold," said Terry in a flat voice.

Kurt wrapped Terry in a cape he grabbed from her rack. "You'll be okay," the director said gently.

A few minutes later Tim returned, saying the door to the storeroom with the flash powder was forced open. "Some of the powder was taken, but I can't tell how much," he added.

"Hey, check this out," Joe said, pointing up.

Nancy looked up at the overhead light fixture. A length of thin wire ran from it, along the wall, ending at the blackened mass by the couch. "When I flipped on the lights, an electrical current ran down the wire to the powder. That's what set off the blast."

She turned to Logan. "The dressing room was kept locked. Who had access to the key?"

"Terry has her own key, of course. The only other one was with the doorman all evening," Logan said. "He had it until we got it from him."

"I didn't lend my key to anyone," Terry put in, frowning.

"Maybe someone else borrowed the doorman's key," Bess suggested.

"Tim, bring the doorman here, would you?" Kurt called out.

When Tim arrived with the doorman, Nancy asked, "Did anyone take the key to Terry's dressing room before we did?"

"No," the man answered.

Nancy felt frustrated. This case was yielding no clues at all.

"No one unauthorized, that is," he added.

Nancy stared at him. "You mean, someone *did* use that key?" she pressed, feeling a surge of excitement.

"Yes, but it was all right. I mean, she was entitled. Otherwise, I wouldn't have let her."

"Who was it?" Terry asked.

The doorman acted nervous now. "She told me she had permission, or I'd never—"

"I'm sure you were doing your job," Nancy told him. "Who took the key?"

"Ms. Alford's understudy," the man replied.

"Holly Bartell?" Bess asked.

"She told me Terry wanted her to get something," he continued.

"That's not true!" Terry exclaimed.

Nancy looked around the hallway. Most of the cast was there, watching curiously.

Except Holly Bartell, who was nowhere in sight.

Chapter

Twelve

WHERE WAS HOLLY? Nancy wondered. The actress had said she was going back in to watch the show but hadn't come backstage with the others to see why the rehearsal had been stopped. Nancy needed to talk to her, but first, she had to get rid of the crowd.

Turning to Kurt, Nancy asked, "Can you have everyone clear this hallway, please?"

Kurt nodded. "Good idea." He clapped his hands. "Everyone, clear out. We'll let you know what's going on in a few minutes."

Nancy stopped the stage manager as he turned

to leave. "Tim, would you stay? We may need you."

"Sure," he replied. Cast and crew drifted off in small groups, talking quietly among themselves.

"We'll get out of the way, too," offered Frank. "Unless you need us, that is."

With a grateful smile, Nancy said, "Thanks, guys, not right now. Bess and I will look for you later."

"You got it," Joe agreed. He motioned to Pat to join him and Frank.

Pat turned nervously to Terry. "You want me to stick around, babe?" he asked.

"Go ahead," she told him. "I'll be all right."

When Nancy, Bess, Terry, Kurt, and Tim were finally alone, Nancy asked, "Where can we sit and talk?"

"Is my office okay?" Tim asked.

"Good enough," Nancy replied.

Tim led them down a flight of steps. He stopped at the bottom, next to a steel door. "The flash powder is kept in there," he said.

Nancy noted the scratches around the lock. "You were right about the lock being picked," she said.

The group continued down a hall that ended at a wooden door, which Tim unlocked. Inside was a plain, windowless room containing some scarred wooden desks and chairs.

"I'm wondering where some people were just

now," Nancy began after they sat. "Like Stuart Firman, for instance."

Kurt spoke up. "He's at the hotel, rescoring some music. That's where his synthesizer is."

"Holly's the one I wonder about," Bess spoke up. "She didn't want us to go into Terry's dressing room, which is pretty suspicious."

"We'd better talk to her right away," Nancy said.

"I'll find her," Tim offered.

After he left the room, Nancy asked Terry, "When did you last use your dressing room tonight?"

Terry knit her brow, concentrating. "Let's see, an hour and a half ago," she said. "At the end of Act One."

"You and Holly don't get along, do you?" Bess asked.

Terry said, "That's putting it mildly. Ever since rehearsals started, she's made it clear that the show would be better off with a *real pro* in the lead. Guess who she has in mind."

"But Terry's handled the sniping with real class," Kurt said.

"Thanks, Kurt," Terry said. "It's not that I don't like Holly, even though I don't. It's more that I don't *trust* her. She—"

At that moment Tim came in with Holly. "She was in the greenroom," he said.

Nancy saw anger in Holly's face. "What is this?

Why was I hauled down here?" Holly demanded, crossing her arms defiantly.

Nancy gestured to a chair. "Why don't you sit down? I have a few questions for you."

"I'll stand," Holly snapped. "And who are you to ask me questions, anyway?"

Before Nancy could answer, Terry burst out, "Why were you in my dressing room? You have no business being there."

The understudy glared at Terry. "Who says I was?"

"The doorman says you took the key and told him you were doing an errand for Terry," Nancy replied calmly.

"Which was a lie," Terry added.

"Terry, please let me handle this," Nancy said gently. "Holly, do you know about the booby trap in Terry's dressing room tonight?" Nancy went on.

Holly shrugged. "I heard," she replied.

"What were you doing there?" Bess asked.

"Not planting a bomb, that's for sure!" Holly stared at Nancy in disbelief. "You think it was me?"

Nancy repeated the question. "What *were* you doing?"

Holly threw up her hands in mock surrender. "Okay, I confess! I wanted to practice the dream sequence, so I borrowed that gauzy cape Beauty wears. And, no, I didn't leave a bomb while I was in there."

Nancy wasn't sure whether to believe her or not. "When did you get the key, and for how long?" Nancy asked.

"I took the costume just after the second act started, and worked with it for about twenty minutes."

"So why didn't the booby trap go off when you went in?" Bess asked.

"Did you turn the lights on in the dressing room?" Nancy asked.

"Nope," Holly replied. "I could see well enough with the light from the hall."

"So, because you didn't turn the lights on, the bomb wasn't triggered," Kurt remarked.

"She's *so* sneaky," Terry muttered.

"If you offered to share, I wouldn't have to sneak around," Holly snapped.

"You can't stand it that I'm the star!" Terry shouted. "You'd do *anything* to get rid of me."

"Cut it out." Kurt stood and held up his arms. "We're just getting information, not making accusations, right, Nancy?"

"That's right," Nancy agreed. "Yelling won't help anything."

"Any more questions for Holly?" Kurt asked.

"Not right now," Nancy said, frustrated because she was back at square one.

"Okay," said the director, acting relieved. "Holly, you can go back upstairs."

The understudy stalked out without a word.

"Let's get back to work," Terry said.

Kurt's jaw fell open. "Hold on a minute. You sure you're up to it? I would have thought—"

"We haven't done the finale, and this is our last dress rehearsal."

"I admire your determination," Kurt began, "but it might be a good idea to let Holly step in for a day or two. After all, we're not going to have our official opening until after several preview performances."

"I can do it," Terry said simply.

After a long moment Kurt shrugged. "If you say so. Tim, can we go in ten minutes?"

"I'll set it up," Tim said.

"That's the spirit," Nancy said to Terry, determined that nothing would stop her from tracking down Terry's attacker.

"I'm exhausted," Terry said forty-five minutes later as she began smearing cold cream on her face. "But I needed to finish that run-through."

"How did it go?" Bess asked. She and Nancy had remained in the dressing room to make sure no one tried to sabotage Terry again.

Terry began wiping off the cream with tissues. "It wasn't brilliant, but there were no mistakes."

Just then Logan appeared at the door. "Can I come in?" he asked.

Terry glanced at him in the mirror and nodded.

"I heard about what happened here earlier," he said, turning to Nancy. "Isn't it your responsibility to prevent attacks like that from happening?"

Before Nancy could say anything, Terry spoke up. "Nancy can't be everywhere at once, can she?"

"Exactly," Logan replied. "You're in a vulnerable position, Terry, and that's why I'm so worried."

"Give me a break!" Terry demanded. She grimaced and pointed at his shirt. "By the way, you've got a gross stain on your shirt."

Terry was so fed up with her manager that she was hitting him with all kinds of criticism now. Nancy wished she wasn't witnessing this fight.

Logan glanced down at the oily patch on his chest. "I was working on your press kit, and I spilled some gunk from the supply closet."

Just then Kurt came into the dressing room, a sheaf of papers under one arm. "I'm glad you saw the rehearsal through, Terry. You were great. All ready for our preview audience tomorrow night. I only have one note for you this time: don't show up here till six P.M. Have some fun during the

day—director's orders. Good night, everyone."
He walked out, leafing through the papers.

"I'll be in the lot when you're ready to go, Ter,"
Logan offered.

Terry shook her head. "I'll catch a ride with
Nancy and Bess," she said coolly.

Logan looked surprised. "But—I thought we
could talk, you know?"

Terry shut her eyes and sighed. "I don't feel
like it right now, Logan. I'm too tired, and I'd
rather go with the girls. All right?"

Logan started to argue but then just shrugged.
"Fine, suit yourself," he said, and walked out of
the dressing room without another word.

Nancy and Bess left with Terry and met up
with Pat and the Hardys.

"You are absolutely fantastic, Ter," Pat said,
hugging her.

"Thanks, Pat," Terry said, smiling up at him.

"I'd like to hang out, but I've got to get back.
Big match tomorrow! Come on, I'll walk you to
the parking lot."

Leese and Cal were standing in the lot. "I'm
not ready to go home yet," Leese was saying. "I
guess I'm still a little shaken up."

"Why don't you come back to the hotel with
us?" Bess suggested. "You can cool out there, and
when you're ready, we'll take you home."

Leese gave her a grateful smile. "You don't
mind?"

"Not a bit," Nancy assured her.

A horn honked and they turned to see a white van pause near them on its way out of the lot. Logan stuck his head out of the driver's window. "See you tomorrow, Ter!" he called.

After saying good night to the guys, Nancy, Bess, Terry, and Leese started toward Nancy's rental car. "What can we do tomorrow?" Terry asked.

"How about Leese's barbecue?" Bess suggested, an excited glimmer in her blue eyes.

"Hey, that's right!" Nancy exclaimed. "We're invited. We can all sleep late, and later we—"

Without warning a deafening explosion rocked the entire parking lot.

Nancy felt sudden, intense heat. She opened her mouth to scream, but a powerful shock wave, like a giant fist, knocked her to the ground.

Chapter

Thirteen

Nancy's head was pounding as she tried to raise herself up on one elbow. Her ears rang, and she felt sore and bruised.

She gasped when she checked the spot, forty feet away, where her rental car had been parked. It was nothing more than a heap of charred, bent scrap metal now. Someone had blown it up!

"Nan? Don't try to move yet."

Blinking, Nancy realized that Frank Hardy was bent over her, concern in his brown eyes. She saw that Joe was tending to Bess, who was sitting up a few feet from Nancy. Logan was at Terry's side, with Cal and Leese behind him. Pat was

114

standing back by the wall of the theater. If they had been any closer to the car, the blast would have killed them, Nancy realized with a shiver.

"I think I'm okay. The shock of the blast just threw me to the ground," Nancy told Frank.

Frank nodded grimly. "This bomb was meant to kill people."

With Frank's help, Nancy slowly got up and went over to Bess and Joe. Bess tugged at the ripped and dirty floral minidress she wore.

"Hanging around with you is rough on a girl's wardrobe, Nan," Bess said, trying to smile.

Logan helped Terry to the stage door stairs, where she collapsed with her head in her hands. The door had opened behind her, and cast and crew members were gaping at the wrecked car.

"I can't take this anymore," Terry mumbled. "I can't . . ."

"Terry," Nancy said, "listen to me."

The actress raised her head, blinking back tears.

"No one knew you'd be in my car. *I* was the target of that bomb, not you. I must be making progress, because someone's uncomfortable enough to try to kill me."

Seeing Kurt and Tim in the doorway, Nancy told them what had happened. "We have to call the police," she concluded.

"I'll do it right now." Tim moved back inside.

"And I'm going to have a word with Holly,"

Kurt added. "She'd better be ready to fill in for you tomorrow." For once Terry didn't object.

"Hey, Ter, you okay?" Pat asked, moving over and putting an arm around her. She responded with a little nod.

Logan glared at Pat and shouldered past the tennis player to head for his van.

"You did great tonight," Pat said. He seemed fidgety and nervous to Nancy. "Um, you're not hurt or anything, huh?"

"No, we were lucky," Terry replied in a shaky voice. "It's frightening, though. If we'd gotten to the car a few seconds earlier, we . . ." She broke off and looked at Pat, biting her lip.

Just then the cab for Pat, Joe, and Frank pulled into the lot. "Oh, there's our cab. I guess we better get going—" Nancy saw Joe eye Pat with disgust. "Unless you need me," Pat added lamely.

"Go ahead," said Terry, appearing small and vulnerable. "Nan, you don't need him, do you?"

"Not me," Nancy said. "But the police might want to talk to you, Pat. If they don't mind, you can go."

Within a minute, Nancy heard sirens approaching. Two squad cars pulled into the parking lot, and several officers emerged, two in plainclothes. Nancy approached them.

"I'm Lieutenant Givens," said one of the officers, flashing a gold badge. "What happened here?"

Nancy told him about the blast and the events leading up to it.

"Someone meant business," he said. "Hey, Larry!" he called to another officer. "Radio the demolition guys and get them over here, pronto."

Nancy pointed Pat and the Hardys out to the lieutenant. "They need to get to McCallum Island as soon as possible. Can you let them go?"

The detective nodded. "Just let me get their names and numbers, in case I need them later on."

The guys spoke briefly to the police, and then Pat and Joe headed for their waiting cab. Frank held back, pulling Nancy aside.

"One thing bothers me," he told her. "Why did that bomb go off when it did?"

"I was wondering the same thing," Nancy said, frowning. "I mean, why wasn't it set to explode when I turned the key, or when we got in? It just went off on its own."

Frank said goodbye, and Nancy let out a sigh of frustration. She and Bess had been on this case for four days, and they were no closer to solving it than when they'd begun.

As the boat cut through the choppy water to McCallum Island, Frank watched Pat standing at the rail, staring out into the starry night. He seemed withdrawn and worried. "Are you all right?" Frank asked.

Pat slapped the rail. "I have to win big tomorrow. I don't want to just beat Alan, I want to *destroy* him. If I'm off my game, he might—"

"Is *that* what you've been thinking about? Your match?" Joe asked, disgusted.

Pat seemed surprised by Joe's outburst. "Sure," he said. "It's on national TV this weekend. I need to finish him off quick, or—"

Joe eyed Pat and said, "Three people were almost killed tonight, including your girlfriend."

Pat's bewildered expression turned to an indignant scowl. "But no one got hurt. And I have problems too. Someone's out to get me, remember? You're here to help me, not give me lectures. So back off!"

Frank spoke up quickly. "We're all tired. Let's drop it, okay?"

Pat nodded curtly, and Joe walked off.

As the boat docked, Frank saw Butch and Kitty waiting at the pier for them. It was kind of late for a welcoming committee. What was up?

As Pat stepped off the boat, Butch said, "I hear you've got a clean bill of health."

"We've set the match for noon tomorrow," Kitty added.

Pat gave Butch a hard look. "We have business

to settle. Like that bonus you said you were going to talk to Consolidated about getting for me."

Butch's smile vanished. "But—"

"Either I get what I want, or I'm going to develop back trouble after this match and quit the tour," he said, stalking off.

After going with Pat to his condo to check that everything was okay, Frank and Joe went to their own condo.

"Pat is such a jerk," Joe burst out as soon as they were inside. "He treats his girlfriend like garbage, and he's blackmailing Butch. I'm ready to walk right now."

"Whoa!" Frank said. "Maybe he's a creep—"

"Forget the 'maybe.'" Joe flopped onto the couch.

"You just want to walk off the case because you don't like the client?" Frank asked.

Joe lay back wearily and folded his arms beneath his head. "No, I guess not."

Frank called the operator for any messages.

The operator had only one message for them. "We must talk, tonight. I'll be waiting for you in the Palmetto Game Room in the Main Lodge. Gunnar."

Frank relayed the message to Joe, who sat up straight. "What does *he* want? Why the sudden change in attitude?" Joe asked.

Frank was already halfway to the door. "Let's go see."

Outside, Frank enjoyed the coolness of the gentle sea breeze as they started across a large, empty parking lot toward the main lodge.

"Maybe Alan told him I was messing with his gear," Joe said, staring down at the pavement as he walked.

"Could be," Frank said, nodding. "I wish we had gotten the results of the tests on that powder."

Frank blinked as a pickup truck facing them across the parking lot turned on its high beams, blinding him and Joe.

"What's with that clown?" Joe demanded, throwing up a hand to shade his eyes.

"There's another entrance to the main lodge over there," Frank suggested, pointing to the other end of the building. The balmy evening had him feeling too mellow to lose his temper over an inconsiderate driver. He angled away from the truck, and Joe followed suit.

"I hope Alan's not there, too. Talking to Gunnar alone might be less of a hassle," Frank said.

Joe agreed as they reached the middle of the open expanse of pavement. "It's weird. Here we are protecting Pat when we don't like him any more than Alan does!"

Behind them, Frank heard the truck engine start, but Joe didn't seem to notice. "If Alan knew what we thought of Pat, maybe he'd be easier to approach," Joe went on.

"I guess," Frank replied. The truck motor suddenly grew louder. Hearing the squeal of tires on pavement, Frank glanced back over his shoulder.

Squinting into the yellow blur of the headlights, Frank saw the dark shape of the pickup grow larger. It was picking up speed—and aimed directly at him and Joe!

Chapter

Fourteen

JOE! WATCH IT!" As he shouted, Frank grabbed his brother and dove to the right. Frank grimaced as his hip slammed into the pavement, and he and Joe flipped over.

A split-second later the pickup roared by, missing Joe's foot by inches. The boys raised up in time to see the truck take a skidding turn around the side of the main lodge.

"What was *that* about?" Joe shook his head and tried to catch his breath.

"That truck tried to hit us," Frank replied, up and ready to take off. "You all right?"

"I'm okay," Joe said. "Where'd the pickup go?"

Joe was right behind his brother as Frank sprinted toward the main lodge. An instant later they heard the crunch of metal, and Frank stopped so short that Joe nearly ran into him.

"Youch!" Joe said. Twenty yards in front of them the truck had smashed into an old tree. The engine had died, and the driver's door hung open.

Frank cocked his head to one side. "Listen!"

Joe heard footsteps running away from the scene. He and Frank raced in the direction of the noise but stopped when they found themselves facing a dense tangle of undergrowth at the boundary of the resort.

"Forget it," Joe panted, bent over hands on knees to catch his breath. "We'll never catch them in there."

He and Joe made their way slowly back to the truck. "Hey, it belongs to the resort," Joe said, pointing to the door, which had the McCallum logo on it.

"Key's in the ignition," Frank commented, leaning in the open door. He took out a handkerchief and removed the key by its McCallum key ring, careful to handle only the edges. "Maybe there'll be prints on it."

Joe frowned at the smashed truck. "I wonder who has access to—"

"Hey! What are you doing?" an angry voice cut Joe off.

Turning, Joe saw three men in colorful sports clothes approaching from the direction of the main lodge.

"Did you happen to see who was in this truck?" Frank asked the new arrivals.

"I didn't see anyone but you two," one of the three, a heavyset, balding man, replied. "What did you do to that truck?"

"What did *we* do?" Joe echoed. "We—"

He broke off as a fourth person, a thin man in a sport jacket and khaki slacks, hurried up, a flashlight bobbing in front of him. "I'm the night manager," he said. When he saw the wrecked truck, he frowned and shone his flashlight on Frank and Joe. "Looks like you two have some explaining to do."

"We didn't crash that truck," Joe replied, shading his eyes with his hand.

"Then what are you doing with that?" the night manager asked, gesturing toward the key in Frank's hand. Without waiting for an answer, the man snatched the keys from Frank.

"Careful," Frank cautioned. "There may be fingerprints—"

"Who are you, anyway?" the man asked. When the boys introduced themselves and explained that they were with the tour, the manager said coldly, "We're tough on vandalism here. I'm going to see who signed this truck out. You'd better hope it's not you."

He trotted away. The other three men gave the Hardys critical glances before returning to the main lodge. "Hey, wait a second!" Joe called, staring after the night manager in disbelief.

"Forget it," Frank said. "We'll clear it up with Butch. Right now, I want to talk with Gunnar."

"You think he left that message to set us up for the hit-and-run attempt?" Joe asked.

"Him or someone else," Frank replied. He and Joe walked toward the main lodge. They'd gone only a few steps when Frank nudged Joe. "Look who's there," he murmured, pointing.

Gunnar Hedstrom was standing just outside the entrance to the lodge, his expression unreadable.

"We got your message," Joe snapped. "You've got some nerve, pal!"

Gunnar's brows knitted together. "What do you mean?"

"Company's coming," Frank murmured, checking to the left of the lodge. Alan Lassiter emerged from the darkness. His gray running suit was dark with perspiration stains, and he was breathing hard. The look he gave the Hardys wasn't exactly friendly.

He's had time to double back here after ditching that truck, Joe thought to himself. "Where were you just now?" he demanded.

Alan frowned. "Running on the beach."

Joe wasn't in the mood for this runaround. "Want to try taking me on *without* a truck?" he growled.

"What are you talking about?" Alan's eyes narrowed.

"Just you and me, one on one," Joe said.

"Chill out!" Frank said, stepping in front of Joe. At the same time Gunnar held Alan back.

Joe clamped his mouth shut and let Frank do the talking. "Gunnar, did you leave us a message to meet you or not?"

"No way. Why would I?"

"Maybe you wanted to lure us to where your pal could run us down," Joe said, staring at Alan.

Alan acted astonished. "You've got to be kidding!"

Frank described the message they had received. "We were on our way to find you when someone in a truck tried to run us over."

"And naturally you thought it was us, right?" Gunnar said sarcastically.

Frank was getting angry now. "You're logical suspects in the attacks on Pat, and your attitude makes you even more suspicious," Frank shot back.

"Save it for someone who'll believe it," Alan scoffed. "You're just trying to smear Gunnar and me."

"We're just protecting Pat," Joe said, trying to be patient. "You know that."

"Yeah? Well, that's not what Pat says," Alan said.

"What do you mean?" asked Frank.

"You should hear him. 'The Hardys will mess you up good.' 'You'll be sorry you hassled me by the time Frank and Joe get through with you.'" Alan mimicked Pat's voice. "Pat would love to get me out of the way. I stand between him and a lot of prize money. If it looks like I'm guilty of something underhanded, Consolidated kicks me out of the tournament and Pat is rid of his biggest rival. Did he offer you money to frame us?"

Joe caught Frank's eye. What Alan said was a definite possibility, given Pat's personality. "What Pat said was out of line," Frank told Alan. "Our only job is to protect him."

Turning to Alan's trainer, Frank added, "Tell us why Pat fired you."

Gunnar shot Frank a steely glance, then shook his head. "I don't have to talk to you. Come on, Alan, let's go."

"We're not doing such a great job of making friends tonight, are we?" Joe said after Alan and Gunnar were out of sight. "Do you buy what Alan said about Pat?"

"Not really," Frank answered. "It's too far-fetched." He shook his head in disgust. "Can you believe Pat told Alan we'd mess him up? What was he thinking?"

"*Thinking?* Pat Flynn?" Joe raised an eyebrow. "You really believe Pat *thinks?* He just does what he feels like and lets everybody else pick up the pieces."

Frank sighed. "When you're right, you're right. Let's call it a night. I'm beat."

On the way back Joe asked, "So, do you think Gunnar left that message and then had Alan wait to nail us?"

"I don't know. Gunnar didn't exactly cover his tracks by leaving his own name on the message," Frank added.

When they got home, Joe noticed the red light on the phone blinking. "Another message. Think Gunnar and Alan want to take another shot at us?"

Joe rang for the message. "Dr. Walsh has information for us," he told Frank a moment later. "Maybe she got the analysis on that powder."

Joe's pulse was racing as he dialed the number the doctor had left. When a voice answered, Joe said, "Dr. Walsh? Hi, it's Joe Hardy."

"I heard from the lab about that powder."

"Great!" Joe held the receiver so that Frank could listen as well.

"The substance is epsom salts," Dr. Walsh said.

"Like what you soak your feet in?" Joe asked.

"Exactly," Dr. Walsh replied. "A small quantity, taken internally, can cause a violent, if brief, gastric disturbance."

Frank spoke into the receiver. "Dr. Walsh, this is Frank. Did you find out what made Pat sick?"

"Yes. We tested the residue from his stomach. The lab results show that there was only one thing that shouldn't have been there."

"What's that?" Joe asked.

"Epsom salts," the doctor replied.

It seemed as if Pat had been poisoned by the epsom salts that Gunnar had in his bag!

Chapter

Fifteen

ADRENALINE SURGED through Frank as he thanked Dr. Walsh and hung up. "So it looks as if it was Gunnar who poisoned Pat," he said, letting out a low whistle.

"That creep. Let's go talk to him. We'll *make* him tell us the truth now. I bet he and Alan were both in on the poisoning," Joe said, starting for the door.

Something held Frank back. He sat on the arm of the couch, frowning.

"What's the problem?" Joe asked, his hand on the doorknob. "We've got hard evidence here, let's move!"

"Something about this bothers me," Frank began.

Joe groaned. "What do you want, a signed confession? We know Pat's food was poisoned by a dose of epsom salts. I found a jar of what turned out to be epsom salts in Gunnar's bag. Gunnar was in the kitchen where and when Pat's breakfast was made, putting stuff into food. What's the problem?"

Frank wished his brother would cool out long enough to listen. "Isn't it strange that Gunnar's bag was lying open with one jar without a label. The whole thing seems too convenient to me, that's all."

"Of course there wouldn't be a label," Joe grumbled. "What would Gunnar write? 'Poison for Pat Flynn?' Okay, okay," he admitted, holding up a hand. "I see it, too. It could be a frame-up." He moved away from the door and sagged into a chair. "So what do we do?"

"Exactly what you suggested—we talk to Gunnar," Frank said. "I just wanted to point out that we don't have a conclusive case against him," he continued, and dialed McCallum's operator to be connected to the coach's condo.

"Yes, who is it?" Frank recognized Gunnar's voice.

"It's Frank Hardy— Don't hang up! My brother and I want to tell you something. Then, if you still don't want to talk to us, we'll take our information elsewhere. How about it?"

"Must it be now? It is late."

"Believe me," Frank said, "it has to be now. I think you'll want to know this."

There was a brief silence on the other end of the line. "Very well," Gunnar finally said. "I'm at Number Seventeen Seaview Court."

"He's waiting for us," Frank told Joe after hanging up.

Joe scrambled to his feet. "Right with you."

When Frank knocked on the door of Number 17, it was opened by Alan Lassiter. "This is getting old," Alan said, fixing the Hardys with a glare. "What now?"

Frank and Joe walked past him into the condo. Gunnar was standing by the couch, his arms folded. "Say what you have to say," the coach said.

"Okay," Joe replied. "We've found evidence linking you to the poisoning of Pat."

"That's not possible," the coach snapped.

"It's a lie," Alan jeered. "They've got nothing. Kick them out."

Frank decided to try calling their bluff. "You don't have to kick us out. We'll leave," he said, "but first thing in the morning we're going to tell the folks at Consolidated Motors what we've found. At the very least, you'll look suspicious. Maybe Consolidated'll even call in the cops."

Neither Gunnar nor Alan spoke.

Joe shrugged. "It's your call. Good night, and good luck." He and Frank started for the door.

"Wait!" For the first time, Frank saw emotion reflected on Gunnar's face. "I don't know what this evidence is that you say you found, but I did not—I *could* not do anything like that!"

"Not even to someone you dislike as much as Pat?" Frank pressed.

"But I *don't,"* Gunnar insisted. "Pat thinks I feel this way, but he is wrong. When he fired me, I felt relief. He was so difficult, always arguing and complaining. If he had not fired me, I might have quit. But I don't hate Pat, I feel sorry for him."

Frank turned to Alan. "You say Pat has it in for you because you're his toughest competition. But that argument works both ways, you know. If you want us to buy what you're saying, you have to convince us."

"Convince you?" Alan echoed. "How?"

"By talking to us," Joe put in. "Don't stonewall us anymore."

Alan raked a hand through his brown hair. "What if you're just trying to help Pat get us in trouble with Consolidated?"

"If that's all we wanted, we wouldn't be here now," Frank told him. "We'd be talking to Butch or Consolidated, telling them what we've found out."

Finally Gunnar answered for both of them,

"Ask your questions. I don't promise answers to all of them, though. We'll see."

Finally! Frank thought. "Okay. What were you doing by the main lodge before?" he began.

"Waiting for Alan," Gunnar replied. "He was running on the beach, and he was due back soon."

"Didn't you hear the noise when that truck came after us?" Joe demanded.

Gunnar shook his head. "No. I had just come outside when you saw me. Before that I was in the lodge writing notes to give Alan about tomorrow's match. I was concentrating and heard nothing else."

"You have an athletic bag full of bottles and jars, right?" Joe asked.

"Yes. It is where I keep my vitamins and other food supplements." The coach frowned at Joe. "Alan says he found you doing something with it. How did you get my bag?"

"It was sitting out on the locker room floor," Joe said.

Gunnar looked startled. "But I never leave it out. I always put it away. Unless"—he paused, thinking—"that was the day Pat collapsed. Everything was so confused, maybe I forgot to put it away."

"Maybe you did," said Joe, glancing at Frank. Or maybe someone had messed with it, as Frank had suggested. "That's all you keep in there, food supplements?"

Gunnar nodded.

"And everything is labeled?" Frank asked.

"Of course," Gunnar replied. "Otherwise, I could make a serious mistake."

Joe smiled sarcastically. "You sure could. Do you ever use epsom salts?"

"Epsom salts? Of course," Gunnar said. "They're good for soaking sore feet. I keep them with my supplies."

Taking a deep breath, Frank asked, "Where were you when Pat was squirted with that phony blood?"

Gunnar blinked. "I don't remember."

"Enough of this," Alan said suddenly. "It's late, and I have a big match tomorrow."

"Just a few more minutes," Frank said.

"No," Gunnar insisted. "Alan must rest. That's all for tonight."

"What a shame," Joe remarked. "I really hoped you'd level with us completely."

Alan reddened. "Look, bozo, I'm tired, and I don't care *what* you do. Go ahead and tell Consolidated your story. You can't prove a thing."

Frank could tell that the conversation was over. As soon as he and Joe stepped outside, the door slammed behind them.

"Interesting, huh?" Joe asked as they started back to their condo. "We start asking them for alibis and suddenly Alan gets tired."

"It's late," Frank said. "Maybe he *was* tired."

Back in their condo, Frank grabbed the phone. "I'm going to call Nancy and make sure she and Bess and Terry are okay. That explosion before was pretty hairy."

Before he could dial, a knock sounded at the door.

"Now what?" Joe asked, rolling his eyes. "Maybe Gunnar wants to confess to everything."

"Yeah, right," Frank said, chuckling. He opened the door to find Butch Van Voort standing there.

"Hi!" Frank said. "I'm glad you're here. A lot's been going on."

Butch didn't move. "We have to talk."

"Right," said Frank. "We have some news for you, and some questions. But we're making progress, I think."

"Well, you can forget all of that," Butch said, continuing to stand by the door, his arms folded across his chest. What was wrong? Frank wondered. Butch was acting as if he were mad at him and Joe.

"Forget it?" Joe got up from the couch and

joined Frank. "Why? We're getting things done and—"

"Oh, you're getting things done, all right," Butch said sarcastically. "Listen carefully, you two. As of right now, you're fired. I want you out of here first thing in the morning!"

Chapter

Sixteen

Joe STARED AT BUTCH in disbelief. All Joe could think to say was, "You're taking us off the case?"

"But why?" Frank asked.

"Because you cause nothing but trouble. You got the chef at the Seaview Grill so mad he almost refused to cook our meals. Gunnar and Alan say you're bugging them. And now you wreck a truck that Consolidated has to pay for—"

"Wait a minute," Frank interrupted. "*We* didn't do that! Someone tried to run us down with that truck."

Butch's face remained stony. "We checked—that truck was signed out to Joe Hardy."

"No way!" Joe's face was red with outrage. "We've been set up because we're making progress!"

Butch wasn't at all convinced. "You're *off* the case, and that's final. Leave your tournament ID cards with Kitty."

Joe flopped down on the couch while Frank shut the door after Butch left. "What brought that on?"

"Kitty, Gunnar, Alan, and that chef have complained about us. The management here thinks we're vandals, and we haven't done a good job protecting Pat," Frank said. "It's not that surprising."

Joe's reply was swallowed by a huge yawn. "I'm too tired to think about it now. Maybe it'll make sense in the morning."

"I'm going to call Nancy to see how she's doing before I go to bed," Frank said.

"She's probably doing better than we are," Joe muttered. "At least *she* still has a case."

"He *fired* you? Really?" Nancy stared at the telephone receiver, amazed. "So what are you going to do?"

Nancy had had the desk transfer all her calls to Terry's suite, where she, Bess, and Leese were sitting.

"I'm not sure yet," Frank answered her question. "How's Terry?"

"She's asleep. She's feeling better because she said she wants to do tomorrow's preview."

"Is she up to it?" asked Frank.

Nancy sighed. "I think Terry looks more fragile than she is," she said. "Oh, by the way, she won't be going out there to see Pat play tomorrow. She needs her rest. Bess and I are going to keep her company."

"How did it go with the police?" Frank asked.

"Okay. That lieutenant thought the bomb must have been set off by a remote radio signal."

"Sounds reasonable. I'm sure you'll find the guy who did it," Frank told her and said goodbye.

Nancy smiled into the phone. It was nice to have someone who believed in her.

Someone knocked on the door just then and Bess went to answer it. Logan and Kurt walked in.

"How's Terry?" Logan asked. Nancy noticed that there were dark smudges under his eyes and stubble on his chin.

"She's asleep," Bess told him. "You look as if you could use some sleep yourself."

Logan sat in an armchair. "I can't sleep with Terry insisting on putting her life on the line every day."

"We beefed up security at the theater," Kurt told Nancy, sitting on the couch next to Leese.

"From now on, someone will be with Terry at all times."

Nancy nodded her agreement. "Good."

Kurt shot a hesitant glance at the door to Terry's bedroom. "I know Terry's decided to go on tomorrow, but I still don't know about that. She's ready to collapse. So I've asked Holly to be ready, just in case."

"Does Holly know explosives?" Nancy asked. Seeing the surprise on Kurt's face, she said, "She has a motive to get Terry off the show. If she's guilty, she definitely doesn't want me solving this case."

"Blowing up your car is a pretty good way to make sure you don't," Bess finished.

Leese stood up then and said, "Excuse me, but I have to get home soon, or my grandfather will send out a search party."

"I guess we'll have to call you a cab," Nancy said.

"You can use my car," Kurt offered. "I'll stay with Terry until you get back."

"I'll hang around, too," Logan said.

Nancy turned to Leese, grinning. "You can have a ride after all."

"Wow. You'd hardly know we're only fifteen minutes from the city," Bess commented from the backseat. Even in the dark she could see that the city had given way to fields and farmland.

"We'll be at the gates soon," Leese said from the front passenger seat.

"Gates?" Bess echoed. "I'm impressed."

Leese giggled. "Our house used to be a plantation. Like in the movies, you know? My grandfather sold off a lot of the land, but he kept the house and gardens."

"What does your grandfather do?" Nancy asked.

"He owns stuff. Like a construction company, a demolition company, a shipyard, office buildings—" Leese recited.

"He sounds like a one-man industrial complex," Bess broke in.

Demolition? Nancy rolled a thought over in her mind. Beau had easy access to explosives if he owned a whole company. But would he go that far? It seemed far too risky.

"Here we are. Make a right," Leese instructed, breaking into Nancy's thoughts.

Nancy drove between tall iron gates supported by stone posts. A drive lit by ornate lamps disappeared around a curve a hundred yards ahead. Nancy was sorry it was so dark. There were probably beautiful gardens and lawns around. Once they rounded the curve, they passed between a double row of carefully trimmed trees. Ahead, Nancy could see a huge mansion lit by spotlights set low in front of it. Its tall white pillars supported an elegant, classic facade.

Bess whistled. "Nice place you have here."

"It's little, but we call it home," Leese said dryly.

The drive circled to the right of the house and ended at a covered entryway. As she parked next to the entryway, Nancy saw Beau Tolliver standing in the mansion's main doorway.

"Uh-oh," Leese murmured. "Looks like I'm in trouble."

"Do you know it's past one o'clock?" Beau demanded when the girls approached. "Your grandmother and I have been frantic." He broke off as his gaze fell on Nancy and Bess. "What brings you two here at this time of night?"

"They drove me home, Grandpa," Leese said.

"Leese was, uh, unavoidably detained," Nancy hedged. "I'd like to talk to you about why, if you don't mind."

"Now?" Beau questioned.

"It's very serious, Mr. Tolliver," Nancy persisted. "I wouldn't disturb you otherwise."

Beau studied Nancy for a moment. "Very well," he finally said. "Come with me." Leading the way, he moved down a long hallway lined with oil portraits. Pushing open a door near the end of the hallway, he said, "We'll talk in here."

Nancy stepped into one of the most elegant,

sumptuous rooms she had ever been in. The furniture was hand-carved and upholstered in silk. It had to be over a hundred years old, she thought. A fire burned in a huge stone fireplace. Andrea Tolliver was standing next to the fireplace, wearing a heavy robe over her nightgown.

"Where have you been, Felicia?" she demanded, rushing over to Leese. Nancy thought she sounded more worried than angry.

"At the theater. We—"

"You're a willful child, Felicia," Beau cut in.

"Mr. Tolliver," Nancy said gently. "I'm sorry to interrupt, but there's something you ought to know. Leese had a very frightening experience tonight. She's lucky to be here now."

As the three girls told the Tollivers about the smoke bomb and car bomb, Nancy watched the elderly couple's faces, looking for a hint that news of the bomb might not be a total surprise.

Andrea gasped and grabbed her granddaughter's arm. "Leese, you might have been killed!"

"I knew *something* was bound to happen!" Beau's face was white with anger. "Felicia, you *will not* have any more to do with those theater people. They're nothing but trouble."

"Mr. Tolliver," Nancy spoke up quickly, "those bombs were only the latest in a series of attacks. Someone is trying to pressure Terry Alford to leave *Beauty and the Beat*."

"What does this have to do with me?" Beau asked.

Nancy met his gaze squarely. "You hate the show and everything involved with it," she said, deciding to be direct.

Just then a light tap sounded on the door, and Beau called out, "Yes?" Nancy thought he seemed relieved at the interruption.

The butler entered. "Excuse me, sir, you're needed in the study right away," the man said.

"Thank you." With an icy stare at Nancy and Bess, Leese's grandfather left the room.

"Um, I guess we should be going, huh?" Bess said, with an uneasy glance at Leese's grandmother.

"I'll walk you," Leese offered.

"That's all right, Leese," Nancy said. "We can find the way out ourselves. Thanks."

Nancy and Bess started back down the corridor full of portraits. "The sooner we're out of this place, the better," Bess murmured. "Talk about stuffy!"

"It's more than that," Nancy said, frowning. "Beau's hiding something, I just know it."

"But how can you—"

"Shhh!" Nancy said, stopping abruptly. Through the double doors to her right, she could hear Beau's voice.

"Calm down! There's no need for panic," Beau was saying.

"That must be Beau's study," she whispered as she tiptoed closer.

Another, shriller voice spoke up. "I couldn't get near the theater. It was crawling with police! Maybe tomorrow it'll be easier."

Nancy exchanged a meaningful look with Bess. "That's Warren Brophy!"

"It had better be tomorrow," Beau said. "We're running out of time. If we can just get past—"

At that moment Bess took a step closer to the closed doors and caught her toe on an oriental rug. She stumbled forward, and struck the wall with a *thump*.

"What was that?" Nancy heard Brophy say on the other side of the door.

"Let's get out of here!" Nancy whispered urgently to Bess. They turned to run just as the doors were flung open to reveal Beau standing there.

"Eavesdropping is a nasty habit," Beau said in a low voice. "It could get you into a lot of trouble."

Over Beau's shoulder, Nancy saw Warren Brophy eyeing her and Bess. She decided now was the time to confront him and Beau—before they had a chance to *really* hurt Terry.

"Hi, Mr. Brophy!" she called. "I didn't expect to run into you so soon."

She pushed past Beau and went into the study,

Bess right behind her. The room was paneled in dark wood, and two walls were lined with wooden bookshelves.

"This is a nice room," Nancy said. "A comfortable place to hatch a plot—but you ought to get it soundproofed."

Beau strode over to Nancy. "How dare you speak this way!" he said, outraged. "You've worn out your welcome here."

"We won't be long," Nancy said, holding up a hand. "I just need a minute to warn Mr. Brophy that he's getting in over his head."

"I don't know what you mean," Brophy snapped.

"For your information, the theater was crawling with police tonight because someone tried to kill us by bombing our car," Nancy said.

"Maybe you know all about that already," Bess added, her hands on her hips.

Brophy started to speak, but only a croak emerged. He cleared his throat. "I know *nothing* about that!"

"You were caught in Terry's dressing room yesterday," Nancy continued.

Brophy had begun to sweat. "I told you, I was just there for an interview with Terry Alford!"

"Terry says she never agreed to that interview," Bess put in.

"Face facts," Nancy said. "After what Bess and I just heard, you and Mr. Tolliver are both suspects in the attacks on Terry. When the police find out, they'll want to have long talks with you."

"No!" Brophy's voice was shrill with fear. "We had nothing to do with any bomb! We only—"

"Warren! Shut up!" Beau lashed out, silencing Brophy. Beau turned to Nancy. "There's no evidence connecting us with a crime. None. Now, you two had better leave, or *I'll* call the police."

Nancy knew Brophy had begun to crack, but she didn't dare ask anything more. She and Bess would have to find some other way to discover what they were up to.

Nancy yawned as she and Bess rode up in the elevator to Terry's room half an hour later. "What a long day," she said. "I'm ready to catch some Z's."

"I know what you mean." Bess checked her watch. "It's almost two in the morning. I hope Logan and Kurt didn't mind waiting for us."

The elevator doors whisked open and the two girls walked down the thick carpet to Terry's suite. Nancy unlocked and opened the door. "Hi!" she called out softly. "We're back!"

Nobody answered.

Nancy felt uneasy as she looked around. The room was empty. What was going on? "Kurt? Logan?" she called again.

Still no response.

"That's funny. Where are they?" Bess asked, stepping into the living room.

Nancy was too worried to answer. Running to Terry's bedroom door, she opened it cautiously. By the dim night-light in one corner, she saw Terry's head on the pillows. At least Terry's safe, she thought.

"Wait a second," she murmured, taking a step closer to the bed. Something wasn't right. The blankets below the head were completely flat. Terry wasn't in the bed!

Nancy felt her whole body go cold. What was going on here? Where was Terry? Why weren't Kurt and Logan here? And what was on the pillow?

Her pulse racing, Nancy went to the night table, turned on the lamp—and straightened up with a gasp.

A hideous and grotesque human face leered up at her from the pillow. It looked like a severed head!

Chapter

Seventeen

Bᴇss's sᴄʀᴇᴀᴍ from behind Nancy made her jump about a foot in the air.

"*Gross!* Nancy, what *is* it?" Bess yelled. "Where's Terry?"

Just then, the bathroom door flew open and Terry rushed out. She was wearing a bathrobe, her hair wrapped in a towel. "What happened?" she asked.

Terry saw past Nancy to the grisly head. Her mouth fell open, and she started trembling uncontrollably. Nancy ran to help her to a chair in the corner of the room.

"I give up!" Terry said, sobbing. "Logan and Kurt are right. I can't do the show—"

"Hey, it's all right," Bess said, putting an arm around Terry to comfort her.

Nancy returned to Terry's bed to take a closer look at the head. "It's a Halloween mask," she announced, fingering the grotesque, painted latex material. "There's a note, too."

Taped to the neck was a message in block letters: OUR NEXT TRICK WON'T BE A TREAT.

"I don't know how much longer I can take this," Terry whispered when Nancy showed it to her. "Can we please go into the living room?"

Terry fell onto the living room couch and closed her eyes.

"Terry, where are the anonymous notes you kept?" Nancy asked gently. She wanted to compare them to the note they'd just received.

"In a manila envelope in the desk drawer."

Nancy found the envelope and pulled out the earlier threats. "The handwriting's the same," she announced after comparing them.

"What happened to Kurt and Logan?" Bess asked, taking a seat across from Terry.

Terry's eyes fluttered open. "Hey, that's right. Where are they? They were here before I went in for my bath," she said, frowning. "Trying to talk me out of doing tomorrow's preview.

"I had trouble sleeping, so I came in here to talk to the guys. That's when Logan got on my case about leaving the show. Then Kurt said he thought it was a good idea! I got so upset that I decided to take a hot bath to try to relax."

Nancy frowned. What could have happened to the two men? She picked up the phone and asked the front desk to ring Kurt's room. When there was no answer, she tried Logan's number.

"Hello?" came a groggy voice.

"Logan, it's Nancy. Sorry if I woke you up, but I need to see you."

After a pause, Logan spoke, sounding hoarse and woozy. "All right. Just give me five minutes. I'm in Room Five Twenty-one."

When Nancy hung up, Terry said, "Please don't leave me alone," in a small, scared voice.

"I'll stay with you," Bess offered, giving Terry a comforting smile.

Five minutes later, Logan let Nancy into his room down the hall. "What's up?" he asked, rubbing his eyes, still half-asleep.

Nancy glanced around the room: a smiling photo of Terry rested on his bedside table; on the dresser was a large studio portrait of her and three framed photos of men in military uniforms.

Turning to Logan, Nancy told him about finding the mask in Terry's bed.

"She was alone?" Logan burst out. "Where was Kurt? He was supposed to stay with her."

Nancy frowned. "Well, he wasn't there when we got there, and he isn't in his room now. I thought you were going to stay in Terry's suite with him."

"I was so tired, I couldn't keep my eyes open. Terry was in the bath, and I kept nodding off," Logan explained. "Finally, Kurt told me to get some sleep. I took him up on it. I was out like a light as soon as I hit my pillow." He slapped his knee in disgust. "I should have stayed!"

"Take it easy," Nancy said gently. "No real harm was done." Obviously, Logan didn't know any more about the head than she or Bess.

"I'll let you get some more sleep," she said, when Logan let a huge yawn escape. As she moved back toward the door, she glanced again at the pictures on the dresser. She recognized a somewhat younger Logan Chaffee in the photos of the servicemen.

"They're my old unit," Logan said. "From my days in the army, Special Forces."

Nancy was impressed. "Commando operations, things like that?"

"Yup," Logan said. "Well, good night. Let me know if there's anything else I can do."

"Thanks. See you tomorrow."

When Nancy got back to Terry's suite, Bess was in her fold-out bed. "Terry's asleep," Bess told her. "How'd it go with Logan?"

"Apparently Kurt was supposed to stay with Terry," Nancy said, changing into her nightshirt.

"So why did Kurt leave her unprotected like that?" Bess asked.

"Good question," said Nancy. "Kurt seemed to think Holly should take over for Terry. I wonder—"

Bess stared at Nancy. "You don't think *Kurt* is responsible for any of these creepy stunts? He couldn't be. My family's known him for years."

Nancy climbed into her cot, and immediately felt her body melt into the mattress. "Anyway, Kurt's not around for us to talk to tonight. We'll have to wait until morning to get an explanation."

She closed her eyes and spoke with sleep-heavy speech. "Logan has two pictures of Terry. She's the last thing he sees at night and the first thing he sees when he gets up. I think he's in love with her."

"Oh, wow!" Bess said. "So Terry loves Pat, who's a creep, and Logan loves Terry, who doesn't even know it. It's a soap opera!"

Nancy's voice was barely audible as she drifted off. "I just hope it has a happy ending."

* * *

"Uh-oh, look who's here," Joe said the next morning as he and Frank walked into the Seaview Grill for breakfast.

Frank saw Butch Van Voort talking to a woman Frank didn't recognize. He was so deep in conversation that he didn't appear to see the Hardys.

With a shrug, Frank said, "I'm not going to sneak around trying to avoid the guy. Even if he fired us, Butch can't keep us from being here as tourists."

"Right. We're just tennis spectators," Joe said, grinning at Frank. "And if we happen to get in a little investigating while we're at it, well, that's nobody's business."

The two brothers started off across the room to an empty table. As they passed Butch and his companion, Frank heard part of what she was saying.

"We already gave him a substantial bonus, and that's all he's getting—"

"Hey, Frank! Joe! Over here!" Pat's loud voice called out. Frank spotted the tennis player sitting alone at a table by the windows.

The only food in front of Pat was a grapefruit and an orange, both unpeeled. "That's not much to eat before a match, is it?" Frank asked as he and Joe sat down.

Pat shot a suspicious glance around the restaurant. "I'm not touching anything this kitchen prepares."

As the Hardys sat down, Frank asked Pat, "Do you know who the woman with Butch is?"

"Donna Kallas," he answered right away. "She's an executive with Consolidated Motors. I hope he's talking to her about getting me more money."

Frank saw that Kitty had entered the restaurant. "Oh, great," he mumbled. "She's coming over here."

"Hi, Pat." Kitty stepped up to the table with a grin. "What's with the fruit? Watching your weight?"

"Very funny," Pat snapped. "I'm watching my health, actually." He began to peel the orange.

"You know, poison doesn't *have* to be a powder," Kitty said. "Something could be injected into that orange, and you wouldn't know it until—"

Pat dropped the orange as if it were red-hot.

"Oh, have I spoiled your appetite?" Kitty asked, all wide-eyed innocence.

Turning to Frank and Joe, Kitty added, "You owe me your exhibition tour ID cards."

"What are you talking about?" Pat asked, as the Hardys dug out their cards and handed them over.

"Didn't you know? Butch canned your junior G-men," Kitty explained with a malicious smile, and trotted off.

"Butch axed you guys?" the tennis player asked Frank and Joe. "Why?"

"He said we've caused too much trouble," Joe replied. "We made some headway in the case, though. We now know you were poisoned by epsom salts and that Gunnar had some in his gear."

"Someone tried to run us down with a pickup truck, too," Frank added. "It's possible that Gunnar and Alan set us up for the attack."

"I *need* you guys," Pat said. "What if *I* pay your expenses? Would you stick around?"

Frank and Joe eyed each other. It took about a second to decide. "It's a deal," Frank said.

"I can't eat now," Pat said, groaning. "I'm too tense. Anyway, I'm signed up for the whirlpool in a few minutes. Come on."

As Frank and Joe followed, Frank noticed that Butch and his companion had left.

The three guys were headed outside when an older couple in dressy sports clothes came up. "Pat Flynn!" the man said, sticking out a hand. "I'm Beau Tolliver, and this is my wife, Andrea. It's an honor to meet you. We took our boat over just to watch you play today."

"We're giving a party at our estate later on. We'd love to have you come," Andrea added.

"If I can," Pat mumbled. He seemed anxious to be rid of the couple.

Tolliver? Frank turned the name over in his mind. Wasn't that Leese's last name? He glanced at Beau with fresh interest. This must be the guy who was a suspect in Nancy's case.

Joe must have made the same connection, because he asked, "Is Leese Tolliver related to you?"

Andrea gave Joe a frosty look. "I have a granddaughter named *Felicia.*" Turning back to Pat, she said, "We hope to see you later, Pat." Then she and her husband walked away.

When Pat and the Hardys got to the locker room, they had the place to themselves. Opening his locker, Pat asked, "Can you guys set the whirlpool timer for fifteen minutes?"

"I'll get it," Frank called. The timer was on the wall next to the gleaming steel whirlpool. Frank rotated the timer to the fifteen minutes Pat had requested. The machine started with a whir, and water bubbled and eddied around in the tub.

Frank was about to rejoin Pat and his brother when he noticed a pile of high-tech massage equipment on a bench near the whirlpool. He looked curiously at various gadgets, trying to figure out what they were. One he recognized as an ultrasound device. He stooped to plug it into a wall outlet, but saw that both sockets were in use.

"Mmm," Frank said. The first cord led to the whirlpool itself, he saw. He picked up the second cord, trying to trace it.

Pat came into the room, wearing a pair of swim trunks, and headed over to the whirlpool.

The second wire ran up the side of the whirlpool between the tub and the wall. There, the wire's insulation had been peeled back, leaving bare copper wires, which disappeared under the frothing water.

Those wires were hot! Frank realized. As soon as Pat stepped into the whirlpool, he'd be electrocuted!

Chapter

Eighteen

"Hold it!" Frank shouted. Pat was about to lower himself into the whirlpool's hot water.

Frank threw himself at the player and grabbed Pat, dragging him away from the whirlpool.

"Cut it out!" Pat yelled, twisting angrily out of Frank's grasp.

"What's going on?" Joe asked, appearing next to them.

Pat glared at Frank. "Are you out of your mind? You could've hurt me!"

"Not as bad as the whirlpool would have hurt," Frank replied soberly. "Take a look."

He yanked the second electrical cord from its socket. Picking it up, he coiled it around his arm, following it to the other end. "Look where it leads. If you'd set foot in there," said Frank, "you'd have been electrocuted."

Pat's mouth dropped open, and his face blanched. He backed up to a bench and collapsed onto it. "If I'd gotten in, I'd be—*dead?*"

"Or badly injured," Joe said. "The whirlpool's safe now if you want to use it," he added as Frank pulled the end of the wire from the water.

Pat's head shook emphatically. "No way."

"This changes things," Frank said grimly. "All the other tricks were designed to harass you, but this one could have killed you. Maybe it's time we called the police."

"No!" Pat said emphatically. "They'd stop the match. I have to beat Alan today! I *need* a convincing win today. Maybe then Consolidated will come up with more money. I have to play this match."

"It's your call," Joe said. "You're the boss, now."

"The match goes on," Pat said firmly. "I'd better get ready."

Pat stood up, and Joe and Frank followed him back into the locker room. As Pat began to dress, Frank asked, "When did you sign up for your whirlpool time?" Joe could practically see the wheels turning in Frank's head as he tried to reason out who was responsible for the hot-wiring.

Pat put on a tennis shoe. "First thing this morning, before I went to eat." He paused, holding his other shoe. "I hope I get to see Terry before the match. I could use a little extra support."

"We forgot to tell you," Joe said. "She can't make it today. She needs to rest up for tonight's preview."

Pat shook his head in disgust. "Great. The day I really need her, she wimps out on me."

Joe was ready to blurt out an angry retort but stopped himself when Frank elbowed him in the ribs.

Before the Hardys could continue talking over the case, Alan and Gunnar came into the room. They nodded to everyone and then went to Alan's locker, talking quietly together.

"Your little scheme didn't work," Pat said. "See? I'm alive and in one piece."

"What are you babbling about now?" Alan asked.

"We disconnected your booby trap, so you're going to have to play me after all," Pat said hotly.

"Booby trap?" Gunnar repeated. He stared blankly at Pat.

"Right, the whirlpool you rigged to electrocute me!" Pat shouted, his face red with rage.

"You've totally lost it, man," Alan said with a scornful laugh.

Jumping up, Pat lunged at Alan. Joe and Frank barely managed to pull him back. "If I don't get you, Frank and Joe will!" Pat yelled, straining against the Hardys.

"Hey!" Frank said, his voice sharp. "Joe and I will protect you, but we're not your goon squad, got that? Don't use our names to threaten anybody, ever."

"'Scuse me," a voice spoke up from the locker room door.

A guy in his early twenties was standing there, looking uncomfortable. He was wearing a windbreaker with a TV network logo on it. "Um, we're almost finished setting up our cameras," the young man said. "Can we get prematch interviews from Mr. Flynn and Mr. Lassiter?"

"Sure," Alan replied.

The TV man waited for Pat to speak. "Mr. Flynn?" he prompted. "Do you mind—"

"*Yes,* I mind! I'm busy! I'm working, understand? I don't have time for pests like you!"

"S-sorry, Mr. Flynn," the young man stammered. "I didn't mean— I mean, that is—"

"Get out and leave me alone!" Pat yelled.

The young man practically ran from the room. Joe couldn't help feeling sorry for him.

"Charming," Alan said. "You really have a way with the public, Pat."

After Alan had changed into his tennis clothes, he and Gunnar left. Joe saw that Pat was still white faced and sweaty. The whirlpool incident had obviously shaken him. Not to mention the fact that he hadn't eaten.

Joe grinned in what he hoped was an encouraging way. "Good luck, Pat," he said. "We'll be out there rooting."

"Go get him! See you after," Frank added, clapping Pat on the shoulder.

Joe didn't miss the worried look Frank shot him. I know what you mean, Joe added silently. I have a bad feeling about this.

"Kurt still doesn't answer," Nancy said. "No one's seen him at the theater, either." She spoke softly, knowing that Terry was resting in her bedroom.

She glanced at her watch, which read twelve-thirty. "I could kick myself for sleeping so late."

"It's not surprising, considering how late we went to sleep last night," Bess pointed out. She was in front of the living room mirror, fixing her hair in a french braid. "I'm glad Leese's party is today. We could use some fun."

Nancy had been so preoccupied she'd forgotten all about the party. It didn't start for another hour or so, though. "I can't just wait around here," she said. "I'm going to search Kurt's room."

"I just can't see Kurt doing anything as nasty as the things that have been done to Terry," Bess said softly.

"I know Kurt is an old friend of your family, but he did leave Terry alone last night, and I have to find out why. Maybe I'll find some clues in his room."

Bess hesitated briefly before saying, "Well— if you're going, I'm going, too."

"I don't think we should leave Terry alone," Nancy pointed out.

"Oh, right, but you have to promise one thing."

"What's that?"

Bess smiled. "That we can eat something as soon as you get back. I'm starving!"

"Sure," Nancy agreed, laughing. "Why don't you wake up Terry while I'm in Kurt's room. I'll meet you in the hotel café when I'm done. Oh—and don't tell Terry where I'm going. I don't want her to get more upset than she already is."

Nancy called the reception desk to find out what room Kurt was in. It was Number 519, right next to Logan's. Nancy went down the hall to 519 and knocked. She wasn't surprised that no one answered.

She looked up and down the hall to make sure no one was there. Then, taking her lockpick from her purse, she delicately inserted the slender metal instrument into the keyhole. After half a minute of probing, she heard the lock click open.

"Yes!" she murmured, opening the door. She slipped inside and closed the door behind her.

The first thing Nancy saw was that Kurt's bed was made. Did that mean he hadn't slept there, or simply that the maid had already remade it?

Going to the bureau, she began opening drawers, but they held only clothes. She then went to the bedside table, where she saw a disorderly pile of papers. She started leafing through them. Most of the papers seemed to be about *Beauty and the Beat,* but Nancy didn't see anything incriminating.

"Here's something," she murmured, holding up a slip of paper. A note scrawled on it read "Noon rehearsal with Holly."

Kurt had said he was getting Holly ready to perform, in case Terry couldn't go on. Was it possible that the two were working together to *make sure* Terry wouldn't perform?

Hold it, Drew, Nancy cautioned herself. You need proof, not vague suspicions. After all, she still didn't have evidence linking Kurt to the attacks.

Nancy was about to go through the desk, when a noise at the door startled her. Before she could even think about hiding, the door flew open.

Nancy froze as a housekeeper backed in, pulling a cart full of supplies. The housekeeper turned around and jumped when she saw Nancy.

"Who are you?" the housekeeper demanded. Her voice rose shrilly as she said, "You shouldn't be in here! I'm calling security!"

Chapter

Nineteen

JUST A MOMENT!" Nancy spoke slowly to make herself sound self-assured. How was she going to get out of this one? she thought frantically.

The housekeeper hesitated, her finger hovering over the telephone keypad. "This isn't your room," she said, "it belongs to Mr.—"

"Mr. Zimmer," Nancy finished for her. "I'm Mr. Zimmer's assistant," she fibbed. She flashed the housekeeper a bright smile. "He asked me to pick up some things he needs and bring them to the theater."

Nancy's mind was going a mile a minute. If the housekeeper was just arriving now to clean

Kurt's room, that meant Kurt hadn't slept there. But why? Because he was up to no good?

The housekeeper clucked her tongue. "The poor thing. He works too hard."

"That's the theater for you." Nancy grabbed some papers from the top of the bureau. "I'd better get moving. Mr. Zimmer told me to hustle back."

Before the housekeeper could say anything more, Nancy hurried from the room. She let out the breath she'd been holding. "Phew! That was close."

Bess and Terry were waiting at a table when Nancy got to the hotel café. Nancy was glad to see that Terry looked rested, despite her scare the previous night. All three girls ordered hearty late breakfasts of juice, bacon, eggs, and muffins.

"Pat called just before Bess and I came down here," Terry said as she buttered half a muffin. "Boy, was he in a bad mood. He lost his match against Alan today, and I guess he needs cheering up."

"He and the Hardys are going to meet us here in about an hour," Bess added, biting into a forkful of scrambled eggs.

Nancy thought how amazing Terry was. She was more concerned about her boyfriend than herself.

"I've thought a lot," Terry said after a pause. "I'm going to stay with the show, and I'm defi-

169

nitely going to do tonight's preview. It wouldn't be right to quit now."

"I'm glad," Nancy said sincerely. She wondered how Kurt would take this news.

Terry's smile faded to a frown. "Too bad Logan doesn't share my enthusiasm."

Nancy decided the time was right to find out if Terry knew how Logan felt about her. "About Logan," Nancy began. "You say he thinks of you as a younger sister, and that's why he's so protective of you."

"He *means* well," Terry said, nodding. "Every time I yell at him, I feel guilty afterward. But the truth is—he's just not a good manager. He doesn't work well with people in the music business. I made an album that was a total disaster, and part of the reason was that Logan made bad choices—the wrong producer, an old-fashioned musical director. . . . But I find it hard to let him go, somehow."

Bess took a sip of orange juice, then asked, "Did you ever think that Logan's feelings for you might be deeper than that?"

"I don't follow you." Terry seemed confused.

"We think he's in love with you," Bess said.

Terry's mouth fell open as she stared at Nancy and Bess. *"Logan?* But that's— What makes you think so?"

"The way he looks at you," Bess replied, "and

the way he talks to you. Not to mention that he has pictures of you all over his hotel room."

From the expression on Terry's face, Nancy could tell she hadn't guessed the depth of Logan's feelings. "This is a surprise?" Nancy asked quietly.

"Well, yes! When I first started on PTV, Logan asked me out, but I told him I didn't want to mix business and personal relationships. He said no problem, and never brought it up again. I didn't think anything more about it."

Terry chewed contemplatively on a slice of bacon. "But, now that you mention it, there have been times when— Boy, have I been dense! We've worked together since we were kids, and I assumed that he just thought of me as a close friend."

"He probably figured if he told you how he felt, you'd find another manager and he'd be out of your life for good," Nancy said, thinking aloud.

Terry frowned. "I have to talk to him. Logan has to know I don't feel the same way about him."

Nancy finished her breakfast before Bess and Terry were done. Standing up, she said, "I think I'll call the theater to see if Kurt's there. I haven't talked to him about what happened last night yet." She didn't want to say anything about her suspicions of Kurt until she had more information.

Nancy made her call from a bank of pay phones in the lobby. Kurt had been there and gone, she was told. Nancy was frustrated to have missed the director yet again, but the crew member who answered assured Nancy that nothing suspicious had happened so far that day.

"Nancy!"

Nancy turned to see Frank Hardy coming toward her. Pat Flynn and Joe were standing by the entrance.

"Terry told us about Leese's party," Frank said. "We rented a car to take you, since yours got trashed."

"Hang on a minute," she told him. "I'll get Bess and Terry. I heard about the match. How's Pat taking it?"

"Mr. Personality?" Frank groaned. "Not great. Not only did he lose, but he turned every point into a screaming match with the linesmen. It wasn't pretty."

Looking at Pat, Nancy saw that he was frowning, his arms crossed over his chest. She hurried back to the café. "Frank and the guys came to take us to the party," Nancy announced.

"How does Pat look?" Terry asked.

"Not great, actually," Nancy admitted.

"Well, I'll see if I can change that." Terry put on a cheerful smile. "Let's go." When they joined the boys, Terry gave Pat a hug. "Come on, let's go have a good time."

Pat stood stonily silent. He let himself be hugged, but wasn't trying to cheer up.

"Uh, the car's out front, and the barbecue's waiting, so let's hit the road," Joe said.

"Right!" Bess exclaimed. "Let's party!"

Still Pat didn't say anything. Nancy could see that it was going to take a lot to lighten his dark mood. Outside, she slipped into the backseat along with Terry and Pat. Frank drove, and Joe and Bess sat in front with him.

"Want to see the preview tonight?" Terry asked the three guys. "I have house seats for you all. Right up front!"

"Why should *I* go see *you?*" Pat demanded sullenly.

Terry stared at him. "Maybe because you care how my big night goes."

"Joe and I will be there," Frank said quickly.

"Where were you today?" Pat asked.

"I needed to sleep," Terry said, her voice calm and level. "Tonight's preview is very important to me. It's the first time I'll have a real audience."

"I get it," Pat snapped. "I should care about your career, but you can't be bothered if mine goes down the tubes."

"Everybody has bad days," Nancy said. "Next time out, you'll win."

Pat turned to her. "What do *you* know about it? If my so-called girlfriend hadn't been too selfish to get herself out of bed and—"

"Shut up!" Terry shouted. *"You're* calling *me* selfish? Mister Ego himself! Just keep your mouth shut for a while and give everybody a break. I'm sick of you!"

Pat blinked in surprise at Terry's outburst. To Nancy's surprise, he really did shut up for the remainder of the drive.

Fifteen minutes later they reached the barbecue site and were waved to a parking lot. "Leese told me this is a municipal park, but she and her friends got permission to use it for the day," Terry explained.

Bess sniffed the air as they got out of the car. "Smell that food!" she exclaimed.

The tempting aroma of hickory smoke hung in the air, and Nancy heard music coming from a bandstand that was visible through the trees.

As they started toward the bandstand, Nancy was surprised to see Logan emerge from the crowd.

"Hi, Ter," he said, approaching them. "I knew you'd show up here." Nancy guessed he'd been keeping a vigil, waiting for Terry to appear.

"Logan!" Terry said, suddenly nervous. "How did you know about the party?"

"Are you kidding? Everybody in the show's been talking about it."

Pat stepped between Logan and Terry and faced the manager. "Why don't you get lost? I don't even know why Terry lets you hang around."

Logan didn't give an inch. "I'll be with Terry long after you're nothing but a bad memory."

"Logan, don't. Pat, *please,*" Terry pleaded, swiveling her head from one to the other.

"Take off, jerk. *Now,*" Pat growled, ignoring his girlfriend.

Nancy watched in horror as Logan lunged at Pat. They fell to the ground, flailing wildly at each other. A circle of spectators quickly formed.

They have to be stopped, Nancy thought. They want to kill each other!

Chapter

Twenty

"LOGAN! PAT! *Stop it!*" Terry screamed, but the guys ignored her.

Great, thought Joe. "Come on, Frank," he called.

Joe grabbed for Pat, who shook free and threw a right at Logan's jaw. Logan dodged the fist, then punched Pat in the stomach.

Frank jumped in and yanked Logan off the tennis player. Meanwhile, Joe tackled Pat as he sprang up. The Hardys dragged the two fighters apart. Finally, Pat and Logan retreated to opposite sides, glaring at each other and breathing heavily.

"You both make me crazy!" Terry shouted.

"He's bad for you, don't you see—" Logan reached for Terry's hands, but she pulled away.

Terry was so mad she was shaking. "It's not your business. You are my *manager,* period. If you can't accept that, you'll have to go!"

Logan flinched. For a long moment he simply stared at Terry. Then he walked away.

"The guy is a loser," Pat said to Terry.

"Go away," she said flatly.

"What?" Pat stared at Terry. "He jumped me! Was that *my* fault?"

"Yes," she replied, her violet eyes flashing angrily. "I don't want to talk to you right now."

"Oh, you don't, huh?" Pat sneered. "Okay. Fine. See you around." He wheeled around and took off into the park, disappearing into the crowd.

Terry's shoulders sagged, and Joe saw her anger fade to weariness. "Was it that bad today?"

"Bad enough," Joe replied. "It wasn't just the match with Alan, either." He quickly told her about the booby-trapped whirlpool.

"That's horrible!" Terry exclaimed when he was finished. "No wonder his nerves are shot!"

Frank nodded. "When he lost the match, he was really frazzled and he lost it. I'm sure the papers are going to make him look like Frankenstein's monster."

"Where was Kitty?" Nancy asked. "Isn't it her

job to defuse embarrassing situations with the media?"

"She was there," Frank said, "but she didn't do a thing to help. We haven't had a chance to figure out what's up with her."

"We have to find Pat right away," Terry urged. "He can't afford any more trouble, not now. If Consolidated hears he's acting up, they'll kick him out of the exhibition tournament . . ."

Her voice trailed off as Leese Tolliver appeared in front of them. "You made it. Let me show you around," Leese said, grinning. "Come on, follow me!"

"I'll meet you later," Frank said. "I'll go look for Pat," he said quietly to Terry.

"I'll join you," Nancy offered.

While the others plunged into the mob with Leese, Frank and Nancy stood and surveyed the scene. "Let's split up so we can cover more ground," Nancy suggested.

"All right," Frank agreed. "We can meet back here in a half hour."

Nancy picked her way through a group of kids dancing on the grass. As she moved close to the bandstand, she caught a quick glimpse of curly, sun-bleached hair to the right of the band.

"Pat!" She ran in that direction and was breathless by the time she made it to him and tapped him on the shoulder.

"Pat," she said again. "We were worried—"

The man turned around, and Nancy found herself staring into the eyes of a total stranger with curly, sun-bleached hair. "Can I help you?" he asked.

Nancy took an awkward step backward. "Uh, sorry, I thought you were someone else."

She kept looking but saw no sign of the tennis player. By the time she went back to meet Frank, she felt totally discouraged. He, too, had had no luck.

Nancy sighed. "Maybe he took off and left the party."

Just then Bess, Joe, and Terry rejoined them. Bess had a paper plate piled with shredded barbecued beef on a roll and two plastic forks. Joe carried a plateful of pork ribs.

"Try this stuff!" Bess exclaimed, holding her plate out to Nancy.

"Mmm," Nancy said, sampling the beef. It was delicious and tender.

"Ribs are my favorite," Terry said. "But I'm too worried to eat now. Did you find Pat?"

"Sorry," Nancy said, shaking her head. She caught sight of Leese then and called her over. Nancy asked if she had seen Pat.

Leese nodded. "Sure. Too bad he couldn't stick around."

"Pat left?" Bess asked.

"He took off with some girl," Leese replied. Her hand flew to her mouth when she noticed Terry. "Oh, sorry, Terry. Me and my big mouth!"

"That's all right," Terry assured her. "Do you know where they were going?"

Leese rolled her eyes. "Believe it or not, he said something about going to my grandparents' party."

"The girl he left with," Frank interrupted, "what did she look like?"

"Real pretty," said Leese. "Fancy outfit, fair complexion, bright red hair."

"Kitty," Joe said to Frank. "Did you hear anything else they said?"

Leese frowned before answering. "She said Butch had what he was asking for, and he'd give it to him later today. And—" She darted an uneasy look at Terry. "Maybe I should stop now."

"I think we'd better hear it all," Frank urged.

"Well, she got real close to him and said she wished they could be friends again. And then he said, 'Why not? I happen to be in the market for a new friend at the moment.'"

Nancy wanted to say something comforting to Terry, but everything she thought of sounded trite.

"When Kitty told Pat that Butch had what he wanted, she had to be talking about money,"

Frank said. Turning to the girls, he explained, "Pat's threatening to walk away from the tour unless the sponsor forks over more money."

"But this morning, the woman from Consolidated said there wouldn't *be* any more money," Joe pointed out. He shot his brother a troubled look. "We'd better go after them and find out what's going on here," he said. "I mean, Pat did hire us to protect him."

"We'll go along," Nancy said. Bess and Terry nodded their agreement. "Leese, your party is great, but we have to leave."

"Sure. I hope everything's okay," Leese replied. "See you at tonight's preview of *Beauty and the Beat.*"

She smiled at Terry, but Joe noticed that Terry didn't smile back. She was obviously worried about her boyfriend, and Joe had to admit that he was, too. He just hoped they got to Pat before there was any real trouble.

In a few minutes they were driving to the Tolliver estate, with Frank at the wheel. Nancy sat next to him with directions that Leese had provided.

"Doesn't it seem strange that Kitty wants to get back together with Pat?" Nancy asked. "Their breakup sounded pretty final to me."

Joe had been wondering the same thing. "She

acts like she hates him," he said from the backseat. "You should've seen the way she needled him this morning."

"She *did* hate him," Terry said, staring out the window. "But maybe she had a change of heart."

Frank was doubtful. "Maybe, but this would be the most sudden one I've ever seen."

"Something doesn't compute," Joe said. "Something I can't quite bring to mind." He settled back against his seat, frowning.

"We're here," Nancy said when the iron gates came into sight.

They rounded the final curve in the driveway, where a uniformed parking attendant waited. They got out, and the attendant gave them a ticket, then drove the car off to park it.

Following a couple who arrived just ahead of them, the teens wound around the side of the mansion. "This place is unbelievable!" Joe said.

On the far side of the house a huge striped awning shading a buffet table and a dozen or so tables had been set up. A band played and couples danced on a portable wooden floor. Farther off Nancy could see a rose garden in full flower framing a river at the far edge of the lawn.

"That must be the Ashley River," Frank said. "Apparently all the plantations in Charleston lined the river, which empties into the harbor."

"Pretty impressive," Bess commented. She

tugged on her pink T-shirt. "I wish I'd worn something fancier."

The crowd was mostly older, Nancy noticed, and they were dressed in more formal clothes. As they wound through the tables beneath the awning, none of them saw Pat anywhere.

"Terry!"

Nancy turned to see Logan jump up from a table where he was sitting by himself. "Am I glad to see you!" He raised his hands in a pleading gesture. "What can I say? I'm really sorry, Ter. I just lost my head. Can you forgive me?"

Terry opened her arms, and Logan rushed over to hug her. "I don't let go of old friends that easily," she said, studying him curiously. "But what are you doing here?"

"I happened to meet Beau Tolliver downtown and he invited me," Logan said. "Where's Pat? I'd like to square things with him, if he'll let me."

Terry's smile faded. "Pat isn't with us."

"We hoped he might be here," Nancy added. "You haven't seen him?"

"No, but that doesn't mean he *isn't* here," Logan said, looking around. "This place is enormous. I tell you what, try asking about him at the buffet while Terry and I check out the gardens."

"Sounds good," Frank said.

Nancy stiffened visibly when she saw Beau and Andrea Tolliver appear under the awning. After the last night, they weren't going to be happy to see her and Bess. It took only a few moments before the couple spotted them. Beau strode over to them, his hands in the pockets of his white linen suit jacket.

"Miss Drew, you are no longer on our guest list, and neither are your friends," he said in an icy voice.

"Let me explain—" Nancy began, but Leese's grandfather cut her off.

"Please leave quietly, without a fuss, or I'll have you escorted out."

Nancy was trying not to lose her temper. "We don't want to intrude, but it's vital that we find Pat Flynn," she said urgently.

Andrea Tolliver had come up behind her husband. "We invited him personally this morning. Is he here?"

"We think so, and once we find him, we'll go," Joe promised.

Beau Tolliver considered it for a second. "I'll give you thirty minutes to search for him, but then you'll have to leave."

It took only a few minutes to question the buffet help. None of them had seen Pat, so they moved on to the gardens, where they caught up with Terry and Logan next to a wall of evergreens. More evergreens could be seen through an opening in the wall.

"Any sign of Pat?" Joe asked.

Logan shook his head. "Not yet."

"What *is* this?" asked Bess, patting the ever-green wall.

"Looks like a maze," Frank said, moving over to the opening. "You know, the kind of thing they have on English country estates. These trees form the walls of the maze. I read that people can get lost in them."

"Maybe Pat's inside it," Terry said, biting her lip.

Nancy glanced through the maze entrance. The thick tangle of branches rose above her on both sides to about eight feet. "We could use up all our time in there. Let's save it for last. If he still hasn't surfaced, we'll—"

She stopped. Something in the maze had caught her eye. It was about twenty feet in, sticking out from a narrow opening between two trees.

"Nan? What's the matter?" Bess asked.

Nancy took a few steps inside, and the "thing" came into focus.

It was a pair of legs.

Nancy ran to the legs and stopped, a chill in the pit of her stomach.

Kurt Zimmer was lying there motionless, sprawled awkwardly on the ground. There was an ugly bruise beside his temple, and a trickle of bright red blood ran from the wound into the brilliant green grass.

Chapter

Twenty-One

IS HE ALIVE?" Frank hurried up to Nancy as she knelt to feel for Kurt's pulse.

Nancy gave Frank a weak smile. "He's breathing but unconscious," she told him. "His pulse is good."

"Kurt! Oh, no!" Terry stood between Logan and Bess, staring in horror at the director. She slumped against Logan, who put an arm around her.

"It doesn't look as if he's lost much blood," Frank said, "but we do need a doctor."

"I'll call an ambulance," Joe offered.

"Get the Tollivers, too," Nancy said.

Joe was already sprinting off. "Sure," he called over his shoulder.

"I think I need to sit down," Terry said weakly. Frank stayed with Kurt, and Nancy and Logan helped Terry out of the maze. They sat down on a nearby iron bench. Terry started to cry.

Logan gently put his arms around her. "It's okay," Nancy heard him whisper. "I'll take care of you. I'll take care of everything."

Terry spoke through her sobs. Nancy had to strain to hear. "They win. I'll leave the show, I'll do anything they want, as long as they don't hurt anyone else."

Too bad we still don't know who "they" are, Nancy thought, frowning.

"Ssssh," soothed Logan, stroking her hair. "Take it easy. It'll be all right, just like the old days." Gradually Terry calmed down. Logan said to Bess and Nancy, "I'll take her back to the hotel to rest."

"Good idea," Nancy said, nodding.

As Logan helped Terry up, Nancy studied her with concern. She seemed dazed, and her eyes were glassy and unfocused. Terry leaned heavily on Logan as they walked toward where the cars were parked.

A moment later Joe reappeared with the Tollivers and Warren Brophy. "An ambulance is on the way. I'll go wait for it out front so I can direct it back here." With that, he took off for the main drive.

Nancy looked grimly at the Tollivers and Brophy. All three of them appeared to be nervous.

"This has gone far enough," Nancy said firmly, planting her hands on her hips. "I need answers."

To her surprise, Beau nodded and said, "Yes, of course. Miss Drew, I hope you don't believe that *we* had anything to do with—"

"We know you and Mr. Brophy planned to disrupt *Beauty and the Beat,*" Nancy cut in. "It's time to tell the truth."

Beau looked away from Nancy and sighed deeply. "All right," he admitted. "We *had* a plan, but it wasn't aimed at Terry." He stared uneasily down at Kurt's immobile form. "Or at Mr. Zimmer."

"It wasn't violent, either," Brophy added.

"What were you going to do?" Bess prompted.

The two men exchanged an uneasy look before Beau replied. "We were going to fill the theater with a foul-smelling gas tonight, which would force everyone to leave. I supplied the gas, and Warren was to plant it in the ventilation system."

Nancy caught Bess's skeptical expression. This didn't sound nearly so serious as the attacks on Terry had been so far. Was he making this up?

They were interrupted then by the sound of an

approaching siren. A minute later the ambulance rolled up and two paramedics jumped out with Joe. They grabbed a gurney and followed him into the maze.

Nancy turned back to Beau. "Do you really think I'll buy that story? Leese said she heard you talking about forcing Terry out of the show. If Terry wasn't your target, why were you and Mr. Brophy talking like that?"

Beau seemed confused for a moment. Then he shook his head and said, "That was something completely different. I wasn't even talking to Warren at the time."

"Who was it, then?" Bess asked.

"Logan Chaffee."

Nancy was surprised. "Logan?" she echoed.

Her confusion must have shown, because Beau explained, "He asked to see me. He said that he knew I hated *Beauty and the Beat* and he wanted to get Terry to quit the show. He asked me to get the theater closed by the fire department for code violations. The loss of rehearsal time would add to the pressure on Terry. I said no, of course."

Nancy wasn't convinced Beau was telling the truth. "Maybe you tried to get Logan to help *you* disrupt the show, because you heard he wanted Terry to quit," Nancy said. "Maybe *he* turned *you* down."

"I didn't invite him. My wife did!" Beau exclaimed.

Brophy stepped forward and said, "I admit that Beau and I felt cheated when Southern EXPOsure was handed over to new organizers. Beau is telling the truth, though."

"In fact," Beau said, "earlier today I decided not to—"

"Here come the paramedics," Bess interrupted. The two men wheeled Kurt out of the maze, with the Hardys behind them. A bandage was wrapped around the director's head.

"How's he doing?" Nancy asked the paramedics.

"There's no sign of nerve damage," said one of the men. "I think it's a mild concussion, but the hospital will run tests to make certain."

"Hey!" Bess called out. "Kurt's coming to!"

Nancy felt a rush of relief as she saw Kurt open his eyes. Kurt tried to raise his head but a paramedic restrained him.

"Take it easy," Joe urged the director.

"Let's go," the paramedic said.

"No, wait!" Kurt's voice was raspy and weak. "I have to talk to Nancy."

"It'll keep until you're at the hospital," Frank said.

"No, it won't! Nan! Where's Terry?"

Nancy took Kurt's hand. "Terry was really shaken up when she saw you'd been attacked, so she went back to the hotel. We'll tell her you're going to be all right."

"You have to warn her right away!" Nancy was worried by the feverish gleam in Kurt's eyes.

"You can relax," Bess told him. "Mr. Tolliver and Mr. Brophy are in the middle of confessing right now."

"Tolliver? Brophy?" Kurt stared at Nancy and Bess. "No! You've got it all wrong!" Kurt struggled against his restraints.

Something was wrong here, Nancy thought. What was Kurt so upset about? "What is it?" she asked. "What should we warn Terry about? She'll be at the hotel soon. Logan drove her back there."

"Logan?" Kurt gasped. "But *he's* the one who did this to me!"

Nancy stared at Frank and Joe, who looked as stunned as she felt. That meant *Logan* was behind the attacks on Terry. Beau and Brophy had been telling the truth.

That also meant that Nancy had just sent Terry off in the hands of a desperate and crazed man!

Chapter

Twenty-Two

NANCY FELT a cold knot twist her stomach. How could she have read Logan so wrong!

"What happened last night at the hotel?" she asked Kurt.

Kurt swallowed before answering. "Logan offered to stay with Terry by himself," he began, "so I went off and sat in a diner, wondering whether to use Holly in tonight's preview. Then I finally decided to hold off on making a final decision until I spoke to Terry today and found out how she felt.

"I still couldn't sleep," Kurt went on, "so I drove around awhile and finally pulled over and fell asleep in my car. Then I went to the theater to make sure everything was cool there. That was when I called the hotel and got the message." He looked at Beau Tolliver. "Mr. Tolliver wanted me to come out here."

Beau nodded. "I became worried about Logan after he came to see me yesterday. He seemed capable of violence, and I wanted to warn someone that Terry might be in danger."

"I drove out here," Kurt went on, "but before I found Mr. Tolliver, Logan found me. He kind of popped out of the bushes by the drive. I should have wondered why he was lurking around, but lack of sleep must have slowed down my brain. Anyway, when I told him about the message, Logan said he knew where Beau was, and would take me to him. He led me back to the maze— and that's all I remember."

"*Logan* left that mask on Terry's bed!" Bess exclaimed. "He wrote the note, too, which means—"

"That he must have written the other threats as well," Nancy finished grimly. "We have to get to the hotel before he does something worse!"

"Will you take my car?" Kurt asked. "I have to get it back to town."

"Of course," Nancy said, taking the parking slip from Kurt. "We'll take care of Terry, don't worry."

"We'll meet you back there," Joe offered.

"Great," Nancy said gratefully. "Go straight to Terry's suite. That's where I'm betting Logan took her. If they're there, keep them there. Bess and I will search Logan's room for evidence and then join you."

"Right," Joe said, giving her the thumbs-up.

Within twenty minutes the Hardys had reached the city. "Make a left here," Joe said, checking a map. "I think it'll save time."

Frank pulled the wheel to the right, and the car screeched around the corner. "I hope we get to Logan before he does anything stupid," he muttered.

"Me, too," Joe replied. "At least— Hey, watch out!"

The jagged fragments of a broken bottle lay just ahead of them. Frank cut the wheel hard, and the car swerved to the left.

"Nice move, brother," Joe said. His grin faded as the car began to bump and shudder.

"I guess I spoke too soon," Joe added as Frank pulled over. The Hardys got out to investigate.

Frank groaned when he saw the right rear tire. It was completely flat.

"That's just great!" Frank muttered.

Frank opened the trunk and handed his brother the tire iron. "Loosen the lug nuts while I get the spare. We've got to hurry!"

* * *

"Are you sure Frank and Joe will be there before us?" Bess asked worriedly as Nancy drove down Market Street toward their hotel.

Nancy nodded. "I'd rather not go up against Logan alone, either. He's already tried to kill us once."

"He planted that bomb?" Bess's mouth fell open.

"Demolitions must be part of Special Forces training. Remember the stain on Logan's shirt after the run-through?"

Bess nodded. "Terry noticed it."

"It must have been grease from our car that he smeared on himself while he planted the bomb," Nancy said, pulling the car into the hotel garage.

After parking, the two girls ran to take the elevator to the fifth floor. Nancy knocked to make sure Logan wasn't in his room, then went to work with her lockpick. As soon as the door opened, the girls hurried inside, closing the door behind them.

The room was empty. Nancy frowned when she saw the neatly made bed. "I hope the housekeeper hasn't thrown away any important evidence. You search the bathroom, and I'll look in here."

Nancy checked the closet first, but found nothing linking Logan to any of the attacks. Moving to the night table, she picked up a pad of yellow lined paper. Before she could examine it, Bess's excited voice called out from the bathroom.

"Nan! Check it out!"

Taking the pad with her, Nancy hurried to the bathroom. Bess was holding a black ski mask. "It was under some laundry."

"Logan must have worn it when he made that lights-out attack on Terry at the theater," Nancy said. "Good work, Bess."

The two girls went back into the bedroom, and Nancy took the yellow pad over to the window to study it in the brighter light.

"Hey, weren't all the notes on paper like that?" Bess asked.

Nancy nodded. Tilting the pad, she made out indentations on the top sheet, as though someone had pressed down hard while writing. She peered more closely and the message came into focus.

"'Our next trick won't be a treat,'" she read aloud. "So Logan *did* leave that mask on Terry's bed. This proves he's the attacker." Ripping off the top sheet of paper, Nancy slipped it into her purse.

"I wonder what else we'll find," Bess said as she opened the night table drawer. She pulled out a small flat metal box with a switch on the front face and an antenna on the top. "Any idea what this is?" she asked Nancy.

"I'll bet you could use it to detonate a bomb by

remote control—like the one that blew up our car," Nancy said grimly. "I've seen enough. Frank and Joe must have gotten to Terry's suite by now. Let's bring this stuff with us so we can play show-and-tell with Logan."

Moving down the hall to Terry's suite, they used their key to let themselves in. Logan was sitting on the couch, reading a magazine. The Hardys were nowhere in sight. Seeing the girls, Logan shot them an annoyed look.

"What is it?" he said. "Terry's sleeping now."

"We have to talk," Nancy said. She walked into the room, with Bess behind her. Where were Frank and Joe? They had to be there any second, so Nancy decided to confront Logan with the evidence she had found.

Just then the door to the bedroom opened and Terry appeared, looking much calmer than she had at the Tollivers'. "I'm awake," she said. "How's Kurt?"

"He'll be fine," replied Nancy. "He sent his regards."

Logan became uncomfortable suddenly. "He's awake?" he asked guardedly.

Nancy nodded and faced him squarely. "He told us everything, Logan. Give it up. It's over." Seeing the desperation in his eyes, she quickly added, "Maybe you can plead temporary insanity. No one has been killed. You'll get off easier."

197

"Shut your mouth!" Logan blazed.

Out of the corner of her eye, Nancy saw Bess flinch. Logan was scary.

"Logan!" Terry turned shocked eyes on him, then said, "Nancy, what are you talking about?"

Taking the ski mask and detonator from Bess, Nancy held them out so Logan could see them. "Here are the ski mask you wore when you attacked Terry backstage and the gizmo we think you used to blow up my car. The police will be able to verify this. My guess is, when you realized that Terry was with us, you set the bomb off early, because you couldn't bring yourself to kill her."

"We found them in your room, along with the paper you wrote the threatening notes on," Bess put in shakily.

"Your military records will tell us if you're an expert in demolitions, which will explain the bomb in my car and the smoke bomb in Terry's dressing room," Nancy went on. "And Kurt will testify that you attacked him."

Terry had been listening to Nancy and Bess with a shocked expression. "Logan, *no!*" she gasped.

Logan's face twisted into a grimace of hatred as he continued to glare at Nancy and Bess. Repressing a shiver, Nancy continued. "I bet you tried to frame Brophy by leaving him a message in Terry's name and writing that lipstick message on her dressing room mirror. I can't prove that, but we have lots of other evidence to put you away."

"Logan?" Terry walked slowly up to him. "Why? What did I do to you? What did *Kurt* do to you?"

"I gave you fame and fortune, not Kurt!" Logan spat out. "But with your new career, you didn't need me. I saw the writing on the wall. You wanted to dump me. Was I supposed to lose you and my job without a fight? No way!

"I decided to shut down *Beauty and the Beat* by forcing you out." He shook his head. "But you wouldn't quit. I was going to set another booby trap at the theater this morning. But when I saw Kurt there, I thought I'd take *him* out of the picture instead and wreck the show that way. He never even saw me following him to the Tollivers'. I'm only sorry I didn't hit him hard enough to do the job right."

Before Nancy could react, Logan grabbed Terry's arm and pulled her toward him. "We're leaving."

As Nancy stepped forward, Logan reached under his jacket and whipped out an automatic pistol.

"Nan, *don't!*" Bess screamed.

"Logan, no!" Terry gasped. "Don't do this!"

"Shut up," Logan snapped. He dragged Terry to the door, keeping his gun trained on Nancy.

Nancy was helpless as he reached back to open the door and yanked Terry into the hall. He was getting away with Terry, and Nancy had no way to stop him!

Nancy took a few tentative steps, following them to the doorway. She blinked when she saw two figures approaching Terry's room from behind Logan and Terry. Frank and Joe! They were moving stealthily, and Nancy could tell they had already sized up the situation. If only Logan kept his back to them for another few seconds . . .

Joe gave a silent signal to Frank, and they leapt into action. Joe grabbed Logan's gun hand and jerked it upward, twisting the man's wrist. Logan let out a screech and dropped the automatic. Frank then darted forward and grabbed both Logan's arms, twisting them behind his back. Nancy and Bess ran to help Terry, while the Hardys shoved Logan back into the suite.

"Sorry we're late," Joe said, grinning. "We had a flat tire."

"Well, that's one case solved," Frank said an hour and a half later. "The question now is, where are Pat and Kitty?"

The police had taken Logan away after getting statements. Once Logan was in custody, Terry had called Kurt in the hospital. They had decided to postpone the first preview of *Beauty and the Beat* until the next night. Now the group was sitting in the living room of Terry's suite.

"Maybe they went back to the island," Joe said.

Frank frowned, thinking out loud. "I just don't trust Kitty. I mean, why didn't she intervene when the reporters lit into Pat after the match today?"

"She probably didn't want to," Terry suggested. "She's had it in for him ever since they broke up. Until this afternoon, that is," she added quietly.

"So, you think that when she told Pat she wanted to get together again, she was lying?" Bess asked Frank.

"I think so," Frank answered. "She tortured Pat at breakfast. He was so spooked he couldn't even eat an orange."

Suddenly Joe snapped his fingers. "That's it!"

"What's it?" Nancy asked, leaning forward on the couch.

"I just remembered what's been bothering me all day." Joe leaned forward to Frank. "Remember when Pat picked up that orange? Kitty said, 'Poison doesn't have to be a powder!'"

Frank knew immediately what his brother was getting at. "We never told her what kind of poison it was, yet she knew it was a powder. And how else would she know unless *she* poisoned Pat!"

Bess gave the Hardys a puzzled look. "Why would she do it?"

"To drive Pat crazy," Joe answered. "To torture him, make him self-destruct. It's her revenge for his breaking up with her. She's always at the resort, so she could have trashed his equipment. And the day Pat was shot with that red dye, she could have squirted that water pistol, then backed off and showed up *after* it happened to calm everybody down."

It all made sense, Frank thought. Except one thing. "I don't see how she could have gone into the *men's* locker room without being noticed. So she couldn't have put epsom salts in Gunnar's bag or rigged the whirlpool."

"Maybe she has an accomplice, like Alan," Joe suggested. "Right now, though, I think she's lured Pat somewhere, and that means trouble. We've got to find him, fast."

Joe was right, Frank realized. "They had to go back to McCallum Island. Let's get down to the harbor."

"I'm coming, too," Nancy told them. "After all, you guys saved us just now. It's the least I can do."

Bess jumped up and said, "Don't leave me behind—unless you want me to stay with you, Terry."

"I'll die if anything happens to Pat, especially after the way I yelled at him today," she said, starting to cry. "But I don't know if it's such a great idea for a whole army to troop after Kitty. She might do something desperate. I think I'll stay here." She gave the others a pleading look. "But you have to promise to call as soon as you find him."

"Definitely," Nancy promised, giving her a hug.

"You just missed her," a middle-aged man in denim work clothes said as the Hardys and Nancy and Bess watched the ferry to McCallum Island disappear. "Next one leaves in an hour and a half."

Frank described Pat and Kitty and asked if the man had seen them.

"Redhead, huh?" said the boatman, scratching his chin. "Sure, they were here earlier and left in a cabin cruiser with another guy. They didn't take the ferry."

"Can you describe the other guy?" Nancy prompted.

The maintenance man shook his head apologetically. "I couldn't see him. He was in the cockpit, and the sun was reflecting off the windscreen."

"I'm going to call Butch and tell him what we know. He can watch for Pat and Kitty on McCallum Island," Frank said.

Within half a minute, Frank had Butch on the

line. "What is it? I'm very busy," Butch said. His curt tone told Frank that he was still angry with him and Joe.

"Kitty poisoned Pat's food," Frank said.

"*What?*" Butch shouted so loudly that Frank had to hold the phone away from his ear.

"Also," Frank continued, "we think she's responsible for most of the attacks on Pat. She probably has an accomplice, a guy. We think Pat may be in danger. We wanted you to know."

There was a short pause. Then Butch said, "I misjudged you two. Thanks for the information."

After hanging up, Frank rejoined Joe and the girls. "He's on it, but I want to get out there and help find them," Frank said.

Joe eyed the sleek, powerful boats moored at the marina. Going over to the maintenance man, he asked, "Any chance of renting one of these?"

"These boats aren't rentals," the man replied. "They belong to the city."

"Listen," said Frank. "This is an emergency. Life and death, and I mean that literally."

The man studied the Hardys, Nancy, and Bess for a long moment. Finally he said, "My hands are tied. Now, I'm taking a fifteen-minute break. Excuse me." He walked over to a snack bar at the far end of the marina and stood there, keeping his back to the teens.

"Can you believe it?" Bess whispered. "He practically told us to go ahead and take one!"

Frank was already halfway to the shed near the boats. He opened the door and stepped in. On the wall over a rear counter was a board with keys on numbered hooks. "Ignition keys," Frank said. "And the numbers match the numbers of the berths."

Frank grabbed the first key he saw. *"Dixie Dancer.* It's in berth twelve. Come on!"

A half hour later Frank cut the engine, and they coasted into an empty berth on the island. Not far away stood a cabin cruiser with the McCallum Island Resort emblem painted on its side.

"That must be what Kitty and her friend used," Joe said. He ran over to check it out. It was empty.

Joe scowled. "Now what?"

"I say we find out where Kitty's staying and go there," Frank said.

Within minutes, the four teens had reached the locked condo. Nancy used her lockpick to get them inside. It was obvious that Kitty did a lot of work there. A desk against the wall had a laptop computer and stacks of papers on it. Frank tried the desk drawers while Joe went through the papers. Nancy and Bess went into the condo's bedroom to look there.

"I found a diary," Frank said. "And listen to this!" He turned to the diary and read. "'B. called with job offer and plan. We will settle old scores. Me for my ruined life. B. for his son.'"

Frank held up a yellowed newspaper clipping. "This was folded into the diary with the entry. The headline says, 'Banned Tennis Pro Dead in Crash.'" He held out the article to Joe.

"It's about Neal Ross," Joe said, scanning the print. "The guy Pat had a fight with, the one who was banned from pro tennis for life. This is about that accident he died in."

Joe's eyes stopped at a name near the end of the article, and he had a sudden, terrible realization. "Frank, this gives the name of Neal's father."

"Yeah?" Frank said. "Who is it?"

"Butch Van Voort." He let the information sink in for a moment. "Frank, he must be the 'B' in Kitty's diary. Butch is her accomplice!"

Chapter
Twenty-Three

THE NEWS slammed into Frank. "Butch must blame Pat for ruining his son's life," he said, thinking out loud.

"Then the other man on the boat with Kitty and Pat was Butch," Nancy added.

"Oh, no," Frank groaned. "I told Butch we're onto Kitty, so he knows we're after them. They won't waste any time getting rid of Pat now."

The four teens tore out of the condo. "Whoa!" Frank said, almost crashing into Alan Lassiter outside the door.

"We're looking for Pat, Kitty, and Butch," Joe said urgently. "Have you seen them?"

Alan nodded. "Yeah, and Pat didn't look so great. Did someone poison him again?"

"What do you mean?" Joe asked Alan, worried.

"Butch and Kitty practically had to drag him onto a boat," Alan answered. "He looked really out of it. I figured they were taking him to the hospital in Charleston. Hey, is something wrong?" he asked.

"Call the police," Frank told Alan. "Describe the boat and the people on it. Say that Pat's in serious danger, and we're going after him."

Alan gaped at Frank. "But—what—"

"Just do it!" Joe growled.

The four teens sprinted to the marina. "Quick. Get in the *Dixie Dancer,*" Frank shouted.

"Keep your eyes peeled for that cruiser," Joe called out when they were under way.

Everyone scanned the horizon. "There! Is that it?" Bess asked, pointing.

"Nope, it's a fishing boat," Frank answered.

As they bounced over the choppy water, Nancy felt a sudden hopelessness. How could they expect to locate one small boat in this huge—

"Frank!" she cried out. "Off the port bow!"

A small white dot bobbed a few hundred yards away. Frank steered toward it.

Nancy strained to get a look at who was in the boat and saw a flash of bright red hair.

"It's them! I recognize Kitty!" she yelled.

As they drew closer, Joe saw Butch and Kitty strain to lift something heavy off the deck. "Frank, they're going to throw Pat overboard!"

Pat wasn't struggling. Was he tied up, Joe wondered, or unconscious?

Butch must have heard their motor, because he looked up and saw the *Dixie Dancer* bearing down on him. Dropping Pat back onto the deck, he ran to the cockpit. The cabin cruiser lurched forward, pulling away from them.

"No problem," Frank said, gunning *Dixie Dancer*'s engine. The speedboat shortened the distance to the cruiser. *Dixie Dancer* was only thirty yards back when Frank saw Butch and Kitty try again to pitch Pat overboard.

"No!" Bess screamed. The *Dixie Dancer* was just fifteen yards away when Pat's body went over the transom with a splash.

Frank cut the throttle as Joe kicked off his shoes and cut through the water in a clean dive. He reached the place where Pat had disappeared in a few strokes and dove beneath the surface. A few long seconds later Joe's head popped back up.

"He's got Pat!" Nancy exclaimed.

Pat seemed to be only semiconscious, and Joe had to struggle to keep them both afloat. Frank eased the speedboat toward them.

"Look out!" Nancy called. Frank had had his full attention on Joe and Pat, but now he saw that the cabin cruiser was heading full speed at the two in the water.

It was going to hit them!

"No way!" Frank muttered. Gunning the engine, he surged between the cabin cruiser and Joe and Pat. Butch veered away at the last second.

Frank slowed the engine and turned to Nancy. "Can you take over?"

Nancy nodded and steered toward Joe. Frank tossed one of the ring life preservers to Joe.

"You guys, the cruiser!" Bess called out.

Butch had turned his boat to take another shot at Joe and Pat. "Nancy, get me over there!" Frank called.

Nancy swung about in a tight turn and brought the speedboat right alongside the cabin cruiser. Frank leapt across the few feet of open water to land on the deck of the cruiser. He sprang up and grabbed Butch, pulling him away from the wheel.

"What!" Butch kicked Frank in the shin and threw a right punch. Frank ducked the blow and drove Butch back with a left hook. He finished him off with a solid right to the jaw.

Frank tensed, noticing a flash of movement beside him. He whirled around and grabbed Kitty's arm before she could smash his head with a huge wrench.

Frank let out a long breath and dropped the wrench overboard. Nancy had picked up Pat and Joe and brought the *Dixie Dancer* up next to the cruiser. It was over.

Shortly afterward *Dixie Dancer* was being towed behind the cabin cruiser. While Frank steered the cruiser toward McCallum's marina, Joe radioed for the Coast Guard and the police. Butch and Kitty were securely tied up on the deck.

"Kitty drugged me," Pat muttered, sitting next to them. "They were going to kill me!"

"You deserve to die," Butch snarled. "My son died because of you."

"Your son?" Pat whispered, confused.

"Neal Ross. Remember him?"

Pat blinked, trying to clear his head. "He was your *son?* I—never knew."

"You rigged the whirlpool and planted the epsom salts in Gunnar's bag, didn't you?" Frank asked Butch.

Butch nodded but said nothing.

"Was that you in the pickup truck last night?" Joe asked.

"You were becoming a nuisance," Butch said. "Interfering with our plans."

Pat leaned forward and stared at Kitty. "Do you really hate me that much?" he asked.

"You don't have a clue, do you?" she said, tossing her hair back over her shoulder.

Pat seemed dazed. "But, why would you *kill* me?"

Kitty shrugged. "It wasn't part of the original plan, but when Butch and I realized that the Hardys weren't going to back off this case, we knew we had to get rid of you before they got to us. After the match today I overheard you planning to go to your friend's party. It was easy to arrange to bump into you there. And—well, I guess you know the rest."

"How can they hate me so much?" Pat asked, shaking his head.

"Think about it," Joe said quietly.

"You were sensational! Terrific!" Bess hugged Terry the following night. Swarms of well-wishers surrounded the actress in the greenroom of the Majestic Theater. The first preview of *Beauty and the Beat* had just finished. Nancy had to agree with Bess—Terry was great.

"Fantastic," Stuart Firman said, coming to Terry's side. Kurt was at her other elbow, beaming.

"How are you feeling?" Nancy asked Kurt.

Kurt touched his bandaged head. "The doctors say I can go back to my normal life, whatever that is, so all's well."

"All right! Dynamite show!" Leese Tolliver squeezed through the crowd, with Cal Lipton holding her hand. Behind her were Beau and Andrea.

Turning to the older couple, Nancy said, "I have to say I'm surprised to see you here."

"We had a long talk with Feli—um, with Leese," Beau said, tugging at the sleeve of his suit. "We agreed to try to understand and respect each other's feelings and tastes more. So here we are."

"And, you know," Andrea added, "I liked it!" She smiled as Leese came over and kissed her cheek.

"Hi, Nancy," a deep voice spoke up behind Nancy. Pat Flynn was standing there, wearing jeans, a button-down shirt, and sports jacket. "I just wanted to say I'm really sorry for the way I treated you. I've got a lot of apologizing to do around here."

Pat seemed less cocky, more subdued to Nancy. "I'm glad to hear you say that," she told him.

"Pat!" called Terry. He ran to embrace her. "I was so proud of you tonight," he said.

Nancy didn't miss the surprised look the Hardys gave each other. Apparently, Pat saw it, too.

"I took a hard look at myself yesterday and didn't like what I saw. So I'm going to make some changes, including leaving tennis for a bit."

"What'll you do?" Bess asked.

He shrugged. "I don't know. Go back to

school, maybe. Whatever I do, Terry has promised to stick by me."

"What'll happen to Butch and Kitty?" Terry asked.

"The same thing that'll happen to Logan, I guess," Frank said. "They'll do some hard time."

"Excuse me, Miss Alford?" Warren Brophy tapped her arm timidly from behind. "I wanted to be the one to tell you this. I spoke to a critic from a major news magazine before. He saw the show, and he's going to give it a rave review. He called Miss Alford an important new star of the musical stage."

Stuart's grin spread from ear to ear. "Well, uh, thanks. I appreciate that, Mr. Brophy."

Brophy gave Terry a shy smile. "I hope this makes up for some of the discomfort I caused you. Good night." With that, he slipped into the crowd.

"Hey. An important new star!" Pat quoted. "Isn't that fantastic?"

"Kurt and Stuart have to get a lot of the credit," Terry said.

"Don't sell yourself short," Nancy replied. "You've got determination and plenty of talent. I'm so happy for you."

"I'll tell you something else I have," Terry said. "I've got some fantastic friends. And you and Bess are two of the best."

"Really?" Bess said, grinning. "You know, you could prove your friendship."

"How?" Terry wanted to know. "Just name it."

"Simple. Tell me where you get those incredible outfits you wore on PTV!"

The future is in the stars,
the possibilities unlimited,
the dangers beyond belief ...
in the pulse-pounding new adventure

THE ALIEN FACTOR

A HARDY BOYS AND TOM SWIFT ULTRA THRILLER™

Tom Swift has caught a falling star—a visitor from outer space who is as beautiful as she is strange. But his secret encounter has set off alarms at the highest levels of government. To check Tom out, a top-secret intelligence agency sends two of its top operatives: Frank and Joe Hardy.

But when the alien is kidnapped, Frank and Joe and Tom realize they have to work together. They're dealing with a conspiracy that stretches from the farthest reaches of space into the deepest recesses of their own government. The fate of the country and the planet could rest on uncovering the shocking truth about the girl from another world!

COMING IN JUNE 1993